Angry Army Ants Ambush Alabama

Here's what readers from around the country are saying about Johnathan Rand's AMERICAN CHILLERS:

"Hey! I've read a lot of your boos and I really liked WASHINGTON WAX MUSEUM. It was the best!"

-Olivia F., age 10, Michigan

"I'm your biggest fan! I read all of your books! Can you write a book and put my name in it?"

-Antonio D.,age 11, Florida

"We drove from Missouri to Michigan just to visit Chillermania!" It's the coolest book store in the world!

-Katelyn H., age 12, Missouri

"Thanks for writing such awesome books! I own every single American Chiller, but I can't decide which one I like best."

-Caleb C., Age 10, New Mexico

"Johnathan Rand is my favorite author in the whole world! Why does he wear those freaky glasses?"

-Sarah G., age 8, Montana

"I read all of your books, but the scariest book was TERRIFYING TOYS OF TENNESSEE, because I live in Tennessee and I am kind of scared of toys."

-Ana E., age 10, Tennessee

"I've read all of your books, and they're great! I'm reading CURSE OF THE CONNECTICUT COYOTES and it's AWESOME! Can you write about my town of Vashti, Texas?"

-Corey W., age 11, Texas

"I went to Chillermania on Saturday, April 29th, 2013. I love the store! I got the book THE UNDERGROUND UNDEAD OF UTAH and a MONSTER MOSQUITOES OF MAINE poster and a magic wand. I really want those sunglasses!"

-Justin S., age 9, Michigan

"You are the best author in the universe! I am obsessed with American and Michigan Chillers!"

-Emily N., age 10, Florida

"Last week I got into trouble for reading IDAHO ICE BEAST because I was supposed to be sleeping but I was in bed reading with a flashlight under the covers."

-Todd R., Minnesota

"At school, we had an American Chillers week, and all of the classes decorated the doors to look like an American Chillers book. Our class decorated our door to look like MISSISSIPPI MEGALODON and we won first place! We all got free American Chillers books! It was so cool!"

-Abby T., age 11, Ohio

"When school first started, I read FLORIDA FOG PHANTOMS. Then I got hooked on the series. I love your books!"

-Addison H, age 10, Indiana

"I just finished reading OKLAHOMA OUTBREAK. It was so scary that I thought there was a zombie behind me."

-Brandon C., Florida

"American Chillers books are AWESOME! I read them all the time!"

-Emilio S., age 11, Illinois

"Your books are great! Me and my friend started our own series. Your books should become a TV series. That would be cool!"

-Camerron S., age 9, Delaware

"In first grade, I read Freddie Fernortner, Fearless First Grader. Now I'm reading the American Chillers series, and I love them! My favorite is OREGON OCEANAUTS, because it has a lot of adventure and suspense."

-Megan G., age 12, Arkansas

Got something cool to say about Johnathan Rand's books? Let us know, and we might publish it right here! Send your short blurb to:

Chiller Blurbs
281 Cool Blurbs Ave.
Topinabee, MI 49791

Other books by Johnathan Rand:

Michigan Chillers:

#1: Mayhem on Mackinac Island
#2: Terror Stalks Traverse City
#3: Poltergeists of Petoskey
#4: Aliens Attack Alpena
#5: Gargoyles of Gaylord
#6: Strange Spirits of St. Ignace
#7: Kreepy Klowns of Kalamazoo
#8: Dinosaurs Destroy Detroit
#9: Sinister Spiders of Saginaw
#10: Mackinaw City Mummies
#11: Great Lakes Ghost Ship
#12: AuSable Alligators
#13: Gruesome Ghouls of Grand Rapids
#14: Bionic Bats of Bay City
#15: Calumet Copper Creatures
#16: Catastrophe in Caseville

American Chillers:

#1: The Michigan Mega-Monsters
#2: Ogres of Ohio
#3: Florida Fog Phantoms
#4: New York Ninjas
#5: Terrible Tractors of Texas
#6: Invisible Iguanas of Illinois
#7: Wisconsin Werewolves
#8: Minnesota Mall Mannequins
#9: Iron Insects Invade Indiana
#10: Missouri Madhouse
#11: Poisonous Pythons Paralyze Pennsylvania
#12: Dangerous Dolls of Delaware
#13: Virtual Vampires of Vermont
#14: Creepy Condors of California
#15: Nebraska Nightcrawlers
#16: Alien Androids Assault Arizona
#17: South Carolina Sea Creatures
#18: Washington Wax Museum
#19: North Dakota Night Dragons
#20: Mutant Mammoths of Montana
#21: Terrifying Toys of Tennessee
#22: Nuclear Jellyfish of New Jersey
#23: Wicked Velociraptors of West Virginia
#24: Haunting in New Hampshire
#25: Mississippi Megalodon
#26: Oklahoma Outbreak
#27: Kentucky Komodo Dragons
#28: Curse of the Connecticut Coyotes
#29: Oregon Oceanauts

American Chillers (cont'd)

#31: The Nevada Nightmare Novel
#32: Idaho Ice Beast
#33: Monster Mosquitoes of Maine
#34: Savage Dinosaurs of South Dakota
#35: Maniac Martians Marooned in Massachusetts
#36: Carnivorous Crickets of Colorado
#37: The Underground Undead of Utah
#38: The Wicked Waterpark of Wyoming
#39: Angry Army Ants Ambush Alabama
#40: Incredible Ivy of Iowa

Freddie Fernortner, Fearless First Grader:

#1: The Fantastic Flying Bicycle
#2: The Super-Scary Night Thingy
#3: A Haunting We Will Go
#4: Freddie's Dog Walking Service
#5: The Big Box Fort
#6: Mr. Chewy's Big Adventure
#7: The Magical Wading Pool
#8: Chipper's Crazy Carnival
#9: Attack of the Dust Bunnies from Outer Space!
#10: The Pond Monster
#11: Tadpole Trouble
#12: Frankenfreddie

Adventure Club series:

#1: Ghost in the Graveyard
#2: Ghost in the Grand
#3: The Haunted Schoolhouse

For Teens:

PANDEMIA: A novel of the bird flu and the end of the world
(written with Christopher Knight)

American Chillers Double Thrillers:

Vampire Nation &
Attack of the Monster Venus Melon

AMERICAN
CHILLERS
AMERICA'S #1 SERIES FOR MAXIMUM CHILLS!

#39: Angry Army Ants Ambush Alabama

Johnathan Rand

An AudioCraft Publishing, Inc. book

This book is a work of fiction. Names, places, characters and incidents are used fictitiously, or are products of the author's very active imagination.

Book storage and warehouses provided by Chillermania!©
Indian River, Michigan

American Chillers #39: Angry Army Ants Ambush Alabama
ISBN 13-digit: 978-1-893699-54-0

Librarians/Media Specialists:
PCIP/MARC records available **free of charge** at
www.americanchillers.com

Cover illustration by Dwayne Harris
Cover layout and design by Sue Harring

Printed in USA

ANGRY ARMY ANTS AMBUSH ALABAMA

1

"Bo! Come here, buddy! Want a treat?"

The yellow Labrador looked up from the garbage can he was sniffing and wagged his tail. Seeing me, he trotted happily in my direction, mouth open, his wet, pink tongue flopping loosely back and forth. Bo knew that I always had a treat for him. Today, it was a little bit of my peanut butter and jelly sandwich that I hadn't eaten for lunch.

"Wanna go for a hike in the woods?" I asked the dog as I tossed him the small morsel. Bo gulped it down, wagged his tail, and followed me as I walked up the driveway, alongside our house, past our white metal storage shed, and into the woods. He stopped to sniff the corner of the shed, but quickly caught up to me.

Although he's not my dog, Bo and I have been friends for several months. He's a stray, and I don't know where he lives. Probably in the woods. He has no collar, and he's kind of dirty, but he's very friendly. There are only a few houses near ours, and most of the people who know the dog are nice to him. I've tried to get Mom and Dad to let me keep him, but they keep telling me no.

And they also don't like it when I feed him, because they say it keeps him coming around. So, I have to be a little sneaky when I give him treats. I really wish I could keep him. I think it would be cool to have a dog to keep me company all the time. In fact, I'm the one who gave him his name.

My name is Scott McGillan, but everyone calls me Scooter. I live near Russellville, Alabama. It's not a big city, and me, Mom, Dad, and my younger sister, Elise, live on the outskirts of town where there are lots of woods and a few swamps. We moved here from Birmingham, Alabama a few years ago, when Dad took a job working for a computer software company. The place where he works is only about a mile away from our house, through the woods. It's a huge building surrounded by a tall mesh fence made of wire. I've hiked back to it a bunch of times. Dad, of course, has to drive to work, so he can't take the shortcut through the forest. The road he drives is winding and curvy, and it takes him about ten minutes to get there.

And I like where we live now. I liked Birmingham just fine, because I had a lot of friends who lived nearby. Here, the only friends who live close are Connor Perry and Annie Shepherd.

But the big differences between where we used to live in Birmingham and where we live now near Russellville are the forest and the swamps. I love hiking in the woods, exploring, climbing trees, and catching toads, frogs, and turtles.

With Bo at my heels, I traipsed through the forest, sweeping branches and limbs away from my face. The only trails in the woods are the ones I made, and I know the forest, fields, and swamps well. I've spent a lot of time back in the woods, and I've never gotten lost.

Today, I was headed to my favorite climbing tree. I'm not sure what kind of tree it is, but it has lots of branches, and I can climb almost to the very top where I can see for miles. There's not really much to see except thousands of trees, but the view is pretty cool.

"I need to teach you to climb trees, Bo," I said as I patted the dog's head. "You'd be famous." Bo nuzzled my palm and licked my hand as he wagged his tail.

When I reached the tree, I grabbed the lowest branch with both hands and swung myself up. Bo stopped and looked up at me. Then, he lost interest. He wandered off, sniffing the ground, searching for whatever it is that dogs search for.

Now, before I explain any further, you need to know one thing: I'm a good tree climber. I'm careful, I'm not afraid of heights, and I can climb just about *any* tree.

So, as I was groping branches and pulling myself up through the tree, I was surprised to hear a loud snap, and even more surprised to find a long, dead branch in my hand that had broken from the trunk.

In a flash of hot panic, I quickly dropped the dead limb and reached up to try to grab another branch . . . but it was too late. I had already lost my balance. My foot slipped off the branch beneath me.

Without anything to grasp, I tumbled backward, knowing all too well that I was in deep trouble.

2

If I would've fallen to the ground, I would've broken a leg, an arm, or my back. Maybe all three.

But I got lucky.

I had fallen only about a foot when I slammed into another branch. It broke my fall, knocking me sideways in the air. In a panic, my arm looped around another branch. I was able to grab hold and stop myself from tumbling any farther. I froze, gripping the branch, catching my breath, and gasping for air. My heart was racing. Twenty feet below, Bo let out a bark. I looked down to see him looking up at me, anxiously wagging his tail, his mouth open, his tongue hanging out.

"I'm okay, buddy," I said.

Carefully, I began making my way down the tree. I was extra cautious, making certain that the branches I grabbed weren't dead.

Bo was waiting for me, standing on his hind legs, his front paws on the tree trunk. When I dropped to the ground, he licked my hand and wagged his tail like crazy.

I smiled and patted his head.

"I'm fine," I said. "Just a little slip. Sure could've been a lot worse."

I looked up into the tree and the blue sky beyond and, once again, realized how very lucky I was. I'd been quite a way up. Had I fallen all the way down, I could've broken more than my back, legs, or arms. I could've broken my neck.

Several feet away, on the ground, was the long, rotten branch that had broken off. Instantly, I noticed there were things on it that were moving.

Strange. I hadn't noticed that when I held the branch in my hand. But, then again, I'd had hold of it for only a moment before letting go.

I took a couple of steps closer. Leaning down, I suddenly realized what I was seeing.

Ants. Hundreds of them. Maybe thousands. They were pouring out from inside the dead branch, racing around in mad circles and frantic swirls, creating little ant freeways.

"Sorry about wrecking your home," I said.

Bo looked at me and cocked his head, as if I was speaking to him.

"No, Bo," I said to the dog. "I'm talking to the ants."

Again, I looked at the branch, at the hundreds of ants scurrying all over it, swarming onto the ground and scurrying up and down blades of grass and other small sticks. I marveled at how fast the insects moved. When I was in first grade, I had an ant farm. It was like a very thin, plastic aquarium filled with white sand. It was fascinating to watch the ants build tunnels and climb through them. They were amazing workers, and every day, they created new tunnels and passages.

But that was when I was in first grade. This year, I would be going into sixth grade, and I wasn't all that fascinated by little tiny ants anymore.

But what was about to happen to me had

nothing to do with tiny ants. It had everything to do with *giant* ants, ants that were bigger than me, nearly the size of grown adults. Never in my life had I been afraid of insects.

That was about to change.

3

I was getting hungry, so I decided to go home and grab a snack. My friend Connor, who lives about a mile away, had gone to the hardware store with his dad. I had hoped that he would be home by now. We always have fun when we get together. My other friend, Annie, also lives about a mile away, but in the other direction. She had gone to visit relatives a few days ago, but she was supposed to be coming home sometime today.

Bo followed me through the woods, but when we reached the white metal shed near our house, he took off on his own. Where he went, I hadn't a clue . . . which is why I worried about him. I hoped he didn't eat something spoiled and get sick. Or get hit by a car. He was on his own most of the time, with nobody to look after him. Sooner or later, I knew something bad was going to happen. I hated to think about that.

Before I went into our house, I heard a familiar voice call out.

"Hey, Scoot!" Connor shouted, and I turned to see him riding up our driveway on his bicycle.

"Hey, yourself," I said, with a wave and a smile.

"Is Annie home?" Connor said as he approached me and then stopped, taking his feet off the bike pedals and placing them flat on the pavement.

"I don't know," I said, with a shrug.

Connor leaned forward on his handlebars, looked me up and down, and spoke. "It looks like you've been rolling around in the woods."

"Worse," I replied. "I fell out of a tree."

His eyes brightened. "Really?" he asked.

"Yeah, sort of," I said. "I was climbing a tree in the woods when a rotten branch snapped. I fell, but I landed on another branch, and I was able to grab onto it."

"You're lucky," Connor said.

"You can say that again," I replied. "I was just going to grab a snack and head out into the woods again. Wanna come?"

"Sure," Connor replied.

I went inside, where Mom was putting on her shoes.

"There you are," she said. "I have to run over to Susan's house to help with her computer."

"Is Elise staying?" I asked, hoping that my little sister was going with Mom. If she didn't, that would mean that I would have to stay home and babysit her. Elise is only six, so she can't be on her own. She's a good kid, but I really didn't want to have to stay home and look after her.

"She's coming with me," Mom said.

Whew.

"Connor is waiting outside," I said. "I was just going to grab a couple of cookies, and then we're going to go for a hike in the woods."

"Be careful," she said, standing up and plucking her car keys off the kitchen table.

"I always am, Mom," I said. But there was no

way I was going to tell Mom that I almost fell out of a tree! I certainly wasn't being careful when that happened.

Outside, I gave Connor two chocolate chip cookies and looked around for Bo. Mom didn't know it, but I brought a cookie for him, too. I didn't see the dog anywhere, so I just put the cookie on the ground by the mailbox. If Bo happened to wander along, I was sure he'd sniff it out.

While we walked along the side of the house, past the white metal shed and into the woods, Connor told me all about the fishing trip with his dad the day before. He said he'd caught a bunch of catfish. I wasn't into fishing all that much, but Connor loved it. Last year, he skipped a day of school to go fishing on his own and got into a lot of trouble.

"Where do you want to go today?" Connor asked.

"Let's go back to the big pond and see if we can find any snapping turtles," I said.

"The pond that's close to where your dad works?" Connor asked.

"That's the one," I replied.

"Sounds good," Connor said. "Are there any fish

in it?"

I shrugged. "I have no idea," I said. "But I caught a big turtle there last year. I'll bet he's even bigger this year."

I liked Connor a lot. He's like me: he's not all that much into video games, computers, or television. He likes to be outside, having real adventures, doing real things. Not that I don't play video games or anything like that, because I do. But given the chance, I'd rather be outside, and so would Connor.

Soon, we approached the big fence that surrounds the company where my dad works. In the distance, we could see the sprawling, single-story building. There were a few cars in the parking lot.

Following the fence line, we continued walking until the forest opened up to a large field. At the other side of the field was the pond.

But before we got there, Connor discovered something.

"Look," he said, pointing. "What's that?"

I looked at where he was pointing and saw a large hole in the ground. It was big: much bigger than what a rabbit or a squirrel would've made. This hole was big enough for me to climb into. There was a large mound of dirt circling it. Something big had burrowed into the ground.

We walked over to it. The unearthed dirt appeared to be fresh, and there were strange tracks all around in the soft earth.

"Is it a bear den?" Connor asked.

I shook my head. "I don't think so," I said as I knelt down and stared curiously into the hole. "Dad says that there are black bears around, but they're supposed to be really rare. Not many people see them."

"You're probably right," Connor said. He pointed down. "And those marks in the sand don't look like bear tracks."

I turned my gaze from the hole and looked at the ground. The tracks were like nothing I'd ever seen. The markings were large, bigger than my foot, and looked like they had been made by sharp claws.

Weird.

I stood and looked around. "Well, whatever it is, I don't think it's a bear. Maybe it's a big fox or coyote."

"Must be an awfully big fox or coyote," Connor mused.

"I can't think of anything else that would make a hole that size," I said. "I mean, I guess it *could* be a bear, but these tracks don't—"

I stopped speaking when I realized that Connor wasn't paying attention. He was looking past me, up over my shoulder, into the distance. His eyes were growing wider by the second.

I turned to see what he was staring at.

My jaw fell.

My pulse raced.

My temples pounded.

At the edge of the woods, climbing a large oak tree, was an ant . . . but we were easily fifty feet away from it.

How were we able to see an ant from so far away?

Simple.

The ant was bigger than we were!

"I have a bad feeling right now," Connor said in a trembling voice.

I had to admit that I had the same feeling. Not only was I freaked out by what I was seeing, but I somehow knew that this was only the beginning of something that was going to turn into something really, really bad.

"What . . . what is that thing?" I stammered.

"It's a giant ant," Connor said. He said this simply and matter-of-factly, as if seeing an oversized bug wasn't anything at all out of the ordinary. But I knew by his quivering voice and his wide eyes that he was just as shocked as I was.

While I'd heard about enormous insects that live in different parts of the world, in the rain forests of South America and in the jungles of Africa, I'd never heard or seen anything like this. The biggest ant I think I had ever seen was probably no more than a half an inch long.

And in Alabama, we have fire ants, which are nasty little buggers. Fire ants are really aggressive, and their sting is really painful. A friend from school was bitten by several dozen fire ants when he accidentally walked too close to a colony, and he had to be taken to the hospital.

But fire ants are small, and most of them never get any bigger than a thumbnail.

The ant I was seeing, however, was like a magnified version, a gargantuan beast. Ants, like many insects, have exoskeletons, meaning that their skeletons are on the outside of their body. It made the giant ant look like it was wearing a suit of dark armor, and it shined in the sun like dark red glass.

While we watched, the ant climbed up the tree, crawling along the trunk and onto a long, thick branch. Despite its size, it was every bit as nimble as a squirrel. It even crawled underneath the branch and hung upside down for a moment before climbing right-side up.

"I think I know what made this hole in the ground," Connor said quietly.

I looked down at the tracks in the dirt. It wasn't difficult to imagine the monstrous insect in the tree had been responsible for digging the hole and creating the strange prints.

"Remember that book we read in school last year?" I asked. "The one about those giant crickets in Colorado?"

"Yeah," Connor said. "That was bizarre. But that was a book. It was just a made-up story."

"Well," I said, "nobody's making *this* up. I know what I'm seeing."

"Great," Connor said. "Now that we both know what we're looking at, let's get the heck out of here. There's no telling what that thing will do if he sees us. Ants can move pretty fast."

"Okay," I said. "But we've got to tell someone."

"Who?" Connor asked.

"I don't know," I answered. "Maybe the police.

Someone's got to know. That thing is probably super dangerous. Follow me. Let's go really slow through the field and hope that thing doesn't see us. When we make it to the woods where he can't see us, we can run."

I was about to take a step when I heard a noise.

The day was warm, and a sheen of sweat glistened on my face. Yet, a cold chill suddenly glossed my body.

In the corner of my left eye, there was a movement nearby.

Another cold wave of horror washed over me. This one felt like icy glue, and it made my skin feel sticky and tight. Connor and I turned our heads, slowly, looking down.

Several feet away, a large leg appeared from the hole.

Then, another.

Slowly, cautiously, we backed away. Connor grabbed my arm in terror as we continued to step backward.

Then, an enormous red head emerged from the hole. It was an ant, but it was wearing some sort of hat, some sort of dark brown beret. In one claw, it appeared to be carrying some sort of radio.

In seconds, the enormous insect was out of the hole, in full view. We watched in stunned horror while it raised up on two legs, standing like a human. It appeared to be looking at the other ant that was in the oak tree on the other side of the field.

Then, it turned and looked directly at us. I will never forget the feeling I had when the insect's huge eyes met mine. It was a paralyzing moment, and I stopped moving. Connor, still clamping tightly to my arm, stopped, too.

For the moment, the giant red insect just stared at us. Then, it turned and looked at the other ant in the tree, then turned back to glare at us.

And without any warning, the creature dropped the radio he was carrying. It fell to the ground and landed near one of his feet. The insect then dropped to all six legs . . . and came crawling at us.

5

Connor and I were spellbound. We couldn't move. It was as if every muscle in our bodies had been frozen, tight and stiff, coiled around our bones like wires.

But when the giant ant charged, we were both hit with a jolt of reality that broke the spell. In school, I learned about the "fight or flight" instinct. Animals, including humans, when faced with a threat, have two options: they either flee and get away or stand their ground and fight.

Flight . . . or fight.

Well, we were going to be no match for the

giant ant, I was sure of that. There was no way we were going to stand our ground and try to fight off an enormous, six-legged freak of nature.

So, we took flight. We spun and ran as fast as we could, heading toward the forest. I was too afraid to look back to see where the ant was, as I knew I might miss my footing and fall. Then, it would be all over for me.

However, when we reached the edge of the woods, I *did* manage a quick glance over my shoulder. It was a great relief to see that, although the ant was in pursuit, he wasn't moving very fast.

But now we had another problem: the other ant had climbed down from the tree and was also heading in our direction. Now, we were being chased by not one, but *two* giant insects.

"Let's get to your house!" Connor shouted. "Which way do we go?"

"We'll never make it!" I replied.

"We have to try!"

"Follow me!" I ordered, darting into the woods and weaving around tree trunks.

"Is this the way back to your house?" Connor shouted from close behind me.

"No!" I replied. "We're heading for the swamp! Ants can't swim! If we go in the water, I don't think they'll follow us!"

"I hope you're right!" Connor shouted.

Although Connor and I were making a lot of noise ourselves, breaking sticks and branches as we ran through the forest, we could hear the giant ants approaching. They were snapping twigs and crushing brush, but the sounds they were making were a lot louder than the sounds we were making, simply because the creatures were so much bigger than we were.

Ahead of us, through the mangled tumble of vegetation and leafy trees, I caught a glimpse of the surface of the swamp. Actually, there are several swamps in the forest behind our house. Once in a while, we find alligators, but most of them aren't very big. The bigger alligators are usually found in the southern part of the state.

"There's the swamp, up ahead!" I said as a branch smacked me in the nose. I ignored the sting and kept running.

The ground beneath our feet became soft and mushy. Soon, we were traipsing through gooey mud.

It was hard going, but we forged on.

"That thing is about thirty feet behind us!" Connor shrieked.

"We're almost there!" I said as my foot plunged into mud over my ankles, soaking my blackened shoes.

Soon, our footsteps sloshing through the mud turned into the splashing of water. We had to go even slower, but it didn't take very long before we were in water that was over our knees, then up to our waistlines. This particular part of the swamp was quite deep, over my head in some places.

When the water was chest level, I stopped and turned. Connor did the same. We were both out of breath, heaving and gasping for air in the warm water. Our clothes were, of course, soaked, but this wasn't something I noticed or even cared about at the time.

But the good news was that I was right. Both ants reached the edge of the swamp, where they watched us intently, unmoving, except for their antennae that wavered back and forth like thin, wiry tails. They seemed confused. The ant with the beret seemed to test the water with one of his front legs, but he quickly withdrew it. The other ant began to circle around the swamp, but neither made any more attempts to get into the water.

"You were right," Connor said. "They aren't going to come into the water."

"I didn't think they would," I replied.

"Where do you think they came from?" Connor asked.

I shook my head. "I don't have any idea," I answered. "Right now, if you told me they came from outer space, I would probably believe you."

We stood in the water, watching the ants crawl through the forest at the edge of the swamp. After a couple of minutes, they gave up. Together, they ambled back through the forest. Soon, they were gone.

"Do you think it's safe to get out?" Connor asked.

"Let's wait a few more minutes," I said. "I want to make sure that they don't hear us when we get out of the water. I don't want them chasing after us again."

But while we were waiting in the swamp, another danger was approaching. It had nothing to do with ants, and it had nothing to do with alligators.

About ten feet away, something suddenly broke the surface. Instantly, I knew what it was, and once again, horror rushed through my veins.

Coming toward us was an enormous water moccasin . . . one of the most venomous snakes in Alabama!

6

Once again, we were forced to make a split-second decision.

Flight . . . or fight. Those were our two options. We would either try to get away from the snake, or we'd have to stay and fight.

But there was no way we were going to stand up to a water moccasin. A couple of years ago, my cousin was bitten by a water moccasin, and he nearly died in the hospital. Water moccasins—and other venomous snakes—aren't anything you mess around with.

"Whoa!" Connor shrieked as he saw the dark brown head of the deadly serpent slipping toward us in the water.

"Move! Move! Move!" I shouted.

It was easier said than done. Because we were in water up to our chests, moving was sluggish and slow. In fact, I started swimming and made faster progress, even though it was cumbersome in my clothes and shoes. Connor did the same, and we both crawled arm over arm on the surface. My arms spun like pinwheels, but no matter how hard I struggled, it didn't seem fast enough. I knew I was going to feel the painful bite of two fangs piercing into my leg at any moment.

Finally, my hand struck bottom, and in one quick motion, I stood. The water still came up to my knees, but it was easier to move. Connor stood, and we rushed as fast as we could, thrashing through the water until we were standing near the edge of the swamp.

Behind us, we saw the head of the water moccasin moving back and forth, slipping through the water, heading the other way. Then, it sank beneath the surface, and vanished.

"That . . . that was a close one," Connor said. He was breathing heavily, gasping for air. "I think that's the biggest water moccasin I've ever seen."

"That's the second time we've been lucky today," I said. "Now, let's get out of here. Let's get to my house where we can call the police."

Quickly, we followed the edge of the swamp and then turned and made our way through the forest, in the direction that I knew would lead to my house. My clothes dripped water and my shoes sloshed, but I was barely aware of it.

"Do you think the police will believe us?" Connor asked.

"I hope so," I said. "Somehow, we've gotta make them believe us. Those things back there, those giant ants, or whatever they are, are dangerous. I'll bet they could kill somebody."

I found one of the trails I had made and felt a wave of relief. I knew exactly where we were, and I knew we were only several hundred yards from my house.

But ahead of us, we were in for a surprise.

I stopped suddenly, holding my right arm out to stop Connor. Then, I yanked him to the side of the trail, and we crouched down in the brush.

"Look!" I hissed, pointing through the leafy branches. *"It's another one of those ants!"*

"That one's different from the other two!" Connor said. "He's lighter in color!"

"That means there's *three* of them!" I said.

"Make that four!" Connor said as he pointed up into a tree.

Sure enough, above the ant on the trail was yet *another* ant. He was climbing down a large tree trunk head first.

"At least they haven't spotted us yet," I whispered.

"I don't want to go back to the swamp," Connor whispered back.

"Me, neither," I said. *"Let's just stay here, and stay quiet. Maybe they'll go away on their own."*

"Let's just hope they go off in the other direction," said Connor.

We could hear their subtle motions and movements as they snapped a few branches and twigs while they moved about. But then we heard other sounds. Branches snapping like thunderbolts.

And—

Footsteps.

Then:

A voice.

A *girl's* voice, farther up the trail. We couldn't see her, but I'd recognize Annie's voice anywhere.

"Scooter? Connor? Where *are* you guys?"

"That's Annie!" I hissed.

Just as I spoke her name, she appeared on the trail, wearing cut-off blue jeans and a plain red T-shirt. She was moving slowly, her head turning from side to side, looking for us. Often, the three of us played hide and seek in the forest, and perhaps she thought that's what we were doing now.

But she had no idea of the danger waiting for her.

"Annie!" Connor shouted. "Turn around now! Go back! Go back!"

Annie stopped suddenly. "Where are you guys?" she said. "I can't see you."

"Do as Connor says!" I shouted. "Go back!"

But it was too late. The ants had blended in with their surroundings, and Annie couldn't see them. They were perfectly camouflaged, and she had no idea she was only a few feet from them.

And when they moved, I knew it was already too late.

Annie shrieked when she saw them and covered her mouth with both hands. By the time she turned to run, she didn't stand a chance. She let out a wail as she was quickly overtaken by one of the ants. It seized her in its claws, picked her up off the ground, and curled her body to itself. Then, it dropped down and began crawling through the forest. The other ant followed close behind.

All the while, Annie screamed and shrieked, crying out for help.

But we knew there was nothing we could do. Our good friend had become the first victim, ambushed by two giant ants and carried off into the forest.

7

"We've got to help her!" I hissed.

"How?!?!" Connor whispered back.

I shook my head. "I don't know," I said, "but we have to figure out something. Let's follow them and see where they take her."

"Are you out of your *mind?!?!"* Connor responded. His eyes were wide, and his mouth hung open.

"No, I'm not," I insisted. "Annie is our friend. She'd do the same for us. Let's follow them at a distance. If we're quiet, they won't even know it. Maybe they'll just put her down somewhere."

"Maybe they're going to eat her," Connor said.

It was a grim thought, and as much as I hated to even entertain the idea, I had to admit that it was a possibility. We didn't know what kind of creatures we were dealing with. Oh, they were giant ants, that was for sure. But what were they capable of? What did they want from us? Did they see us as food? Did they see us as a threat? I had no idea.

The only thing I knew was that the longer we stayed in one place, the farther and farther away the ants were taking Annie.

I stood. "Come on, Connor!" I said. "Let's go! We've got to follow those ants and save Annie!"

Connor got to his feet, and we hustled down the trail, moving as quietly as we could. We tried to follow the ants, which meant that we would be stepping through branches and brush. As we hustled along, we tried to make as little noise as possible. Soon, I spotted the gargantuan ants ahead of us, crawling through the forest.

I stopped and pointed. "There they are," I whispered. "Let's keep moving, but not get any closer.

Let's see where they go."

The really terrible thing was that we could still hear Annie shouting and screaming, crying out for help.

That's good, I thought. *If she can scream and cry out, at least she's still alive. If she can continue to make noise, we'll be able to follow her by listening for her voice.*

The ants emerged in a clearing at the foot of the hill. Part way up the hill was a hole in the ground, similar to the one we'd found near the pond. It was quickly obvious that was where the ants were taking Annie. While we watched, the two ants climbed the short slope and vanished into the hole.

With Annie.

"Now what?" Connor asked.

"Now we go for help," I replied. "Now, we know where they've taken her. We can lead the police back to this very spot. Let's hurry!"

Still soaking from our swim in the swamp, we raced home. I wasted no time grabbing the phone and calling the police . . . but no matter what I said, the woman dispatcher wouldn't believe me.

"I'm serious!" I insisted. "Our friend has been

kidnapped by some sort of giant ant!"

"Young man," the woman snapped harshly, "stop playing games. This phone line isn't for jokes. Now, if you call again, you're going to be in a lot of trouble."

I hung up and then tried calling Mom, but she didn't pick up her phone. I left her a message, telling her to call me back, that it was an emergency.

Then, I tried calling our only next door neighbor, Mrs. Simms. She wasn't home.

Connor and I quickly realized that if Annie was going to be saved, it was going to be up to us. We had no choice: somehow, we had to go down into that tunnel and find Annie. Somehow, we had to rescue her and get her out alive . . . if it already wasn't too late.

8

Connor and I were still drenched, and we needed to get out of our wet clothing. He's about my size, so I was able to give him a pair of my shorts, a shirt, and socks. I had an old pair of sneakers, too. They were a little too big for him, but it didn't matter.

Frantic, we hustled into our dry clothing. We knew we had to hurry.

"How are we going to do this?" Connor asked as he pulled one of my T-shirts over his head.

"I don't know," I replied. "All I know is we'd better hurry."

"Do you have any insect killer?" asked Connor.

My mind brightened. "Yes!" I said. I raced into the kitchen and opened the cupboard beneath the sink. Inside, I found a can of insect killing spray.

"We can take this," I said. "The only problem is that we would have to get pretty close to the ants. And they might be too big for the spray to have any effect at all."

"Hey, it's better than nothing," Connor said.

"That's what I was thinking," I replied, stuffing the can into my back pocket. It was a tight fit and a little uncomfortable, but the canister was snug, and I was confident that it wouldn't fall out. I'd be able to grab it quickly if I needed it.

Something else was in the cupboard: a flashlight. It was black, heavy, and about twelve inches long. That would come in handy, too, so I snapped it up and handed it to Connor.

"Hang on to this," I said. "We're going to need it."

"What else do you have that we can use to fight off giant ants?" Connor asked.

I thought for a moment. My mind was racing, and it was hard to focus. Suddenly, something came to mind.

My bow and arrow. I bought it at a flea market the year before. It was old, but it still worked. I had hours of fun at target practice, but I wasn't a very good shot, and I missed the target a lot. Although I had lost a few arrows in the woods, I still had a half-dozen left in a quiver that was attached to the bow.

"I have a bow and arrow," I told Connor. "It's in the storage shed. Come on."

We raced outside to the small, white metal shed. I slid open the door. Inside was a tangled mass of clutter: a couple of bicycles, an ancient lawnmower, a bunch of old, rusting tools, fishing poles, tackle boxes—all sorts of stuff.

My bow was on a shelf on the right, and I grabbed it. The quiver had fallen and the arrows had spilled out, so I gathered them up.

"I'm gonna take this," Connor said, grabbing a garden shovel that had been leaning on the opposite wall.

Armed only with a can of insect killer, my flea market bow, six arrows, and an ordinary garden shovel, we raced into the woods on a mission to save our friend.

Branches smacked at my face and bare arms as we darted through the woods, over logs, around trees, and through bushes. There were several muddy areas that caused us to slow down, but at least we didn't have to wade through any swamps.

Finally, I spotted the hole in the hill, the place where the ants had taken Annie.

"There it is," I said, gesturing with my bow.

We stopped at the edge of the forest, breathing heavily, turning our heads from side to side, gazing at the landscape. I wanted to make sure that there were no ants around.

We stood there for a moment or two, but it seemed like forever. I could hear our breaths heaving, and a few birds chirping in the trees. Other than that? All was silent.

"Now what?" Connor asked as he leaned on the shovel.

"You know as well as I do," I replied. "We've got to go down into that hole."

Connor sighed and flicked on the flashlight. "Okay," he said. "Let's get Annie and go home."

He made it sound like it was going to be simple. Oh, I know he didn't mean it that way, but that's what it sounded like. It sounded like we would just simply crawl down into the ant hole, find Annie, and take her home.

It sure would be great if it worked out that way . . . but it wasn't going to.

"You ready?" Connor asked, gesturing with the flashlight toward the hole.

I shook my head. "No," I replied. "But let's go."

Connor, holding the flashlight in one hand and the garden shovel in the other, carefully slipped into the hole. Carrying my bow and arrows in one hand, I followed close behind. The only thing I could think of was how crazy this whole thing was.

But if things had been crazy up until that point, that was about to change. Things weren't going to be crazy anymore.

They were about to become *insane.*

9

One thing I must admit: when I followed Connor into the hole, I was terrified. In fact, I'm not even sure if *terrified* is the right word, because I was much more scared than that.

But if *I* was afraid, I could only imagine what Connor was feeling. He was the first one into the hole. Even though he had a flashlight and a shovel, he was the first to enter into the ground, into unfamiliar territory. One of those ants could appear at any moment, and there might not be a thing we'd be able to do.

But as soon as I wriggled through the hole, I was relieved to discover that it widened to an area that allowed us to stand up without bending over. I guess I had thought that we would be crawling on our hands and knees, but that wasn't the case.

So, for the moment, we stood our ground. Daylight streamed through the hole over my shoulder, and the darkness ahead of us was dimly illuminated by the glow of the flashlight. Connor swept the beam back and forth.

"I don't see anything," he said.

"Hang on a second," I said. "Don't go any farther."

In the murky gloom, I pulled one of my practice arrows from the quiver. I inserted the nock into the string. Then, gripping the bow, I held it with my left hand and used my index finger to hold the shaft to the arrow rest on the bow.

"Okay," I said. "I just want to be ready. Let's walk side-by-side as far as we can. If any of those things come at us, I'll shoot them with an arrow."

Slowly, we started walking. Connor slowly swept the flashlight beam back and forth with his left hand, and he held the shovel in his right. I remained at his side.

It was a strange feeling to be underground. I guess I had always thought that if I dug a tunnel underground, the walls would be hard-packed dirt. But here, broken, jagged roots hung above us and poked out from every side of the tunnel. Some of them were long enough to hang down and scrape our shoulders. Others were caked with dirt that fell into our hair when we bumped them. I had to blink a few times to keep the sand from falling into my eyes.

Ahead of us, the tunnel turned to the right, but when Connor moved the flashlight beam to the left, we saw yet another tunnel moving off in that direction.

"Which way?" Connor asked, moving the flashlight beam back and forth, from left to right, illuminating each tunnel.

"I don't know," I said, shaking my head. "Shine your light on the ground, and let's see if we can find any tracks. If Annie was able to get her foot loose, she might have left a footprint in the dirt. That would tell us which way they took her."

A quick search of the ground around us yielded nothing except claw marks.

"I'm not sure if we're doing the right thing, after

all," Connor said. "Maybe we should go back and find someone to help us."

"We already tried that," I said. "We called the police, and they didn't believe us. I called my mom. We tried calling Mrs. Simms, but she wasn't home. And even if we did go back to try to find help, it would take time. As it is, it might already be too late."

My words were swallowed by the dark tunnel, and neither of us spoke. Here, in the depths of the underground, there were no echoes, no sounds at all. No birds, no cars. No distant airplanes flying overhead. It was so quiet that I could hear my own heart beating.

And then we heard another sound altogether.

A scraping noise.

Scratching, a scuffle, a movement of dirt.

"Where is it coming from?" Connor hissed frantically.

"It sounds like it's coming from down there," I whispered, gesturing to the right with my bow and arrow. *"It sounds like it's coming from that way."*

We listened for a moment longer, just long enough to realize that the sound was getting closer, that whatever was making the noise was drawing near.

In the glow of the flashlight, there was nothing

to see, but there was no doubt as to what was making the sound.

"Quick!" I hissed as I pointed to the tunnel that went off to the left. *"Let's go this way and duck down!"* Without waiting for Connor, I took several hurried steps.

"What if he comes our way?" Connor said as he followed me.

"Crouch down behind me," I said as I turned and knelt down. *"Get down behind me and shut your flashlight off. We'll have to listen carefully. If I think the thing is getting too close, I'll let you know. When that happens, turn the flashlight on and shine it right in front of us. I'll be ready with my bow and arrow."*

"And I'll be ready with the shovel," Connor said. He slunk around behind me and pressed up against my back. The flashlight clicked off, and the darkness ate us alive.

"Tell me one thing," he whispered in my ear. *"Tell me you're a good shot with that thing."*

"I'm a good shot with this thing," I whispered back. I know it wasn't the truth, but that's not what Connor asked. He told me to tell him that I was a good shot with my bow and arrow, so that's what I told him.

I didn't tell him it wasn't true, that I hadn't practiced much and I wasn't a very good shot.

But I was pretty sure that if an ant came at us, I would be able to hit it, simply because it was so big. It would be hard to miss such a big target that was only a few feet in front of me.

Still, I was scared, and I had my doubts. If I really had to shoot my arrow, would it stop the ant?

As the scraping and scuffling sounds drew closer, I realized that I was about to get my answer . . . whether I liked it or not.

10

It was a terrifying feeling, crouched down in the darkness, unable to see anything. We could hear the giant ant approaching, but we couldn't see him. The only thing we could do was stay where we were and hope that the ant didn't discover our hiding place. There was no doubt that if he turned and looked in our direction, he would be able to see us. Although I didn't know much about ants, I was sure that they were very capable of seeing things in darkness, probably like bats or owls. Unlike humans, many insects and animals are well-equipped to see just fine in low light or even total darkness.

"See anything yet?" Connor asked.

"Nothing," I replied quietly, shaking my head. *"Just be ready to turn on the flashlight if I say so. If I have to shoot an arrow, I'm going to need some light to see."*

Huddled in the darkness, we waited as the scraping sound drew closer and closer. The suspense nearly killed me.

Finally, when I was certain that the ant was only a few feet away, I almost let my arrow fly out of sheer panic. I knew that the ant was right in front of me in the darkness.

But I held back. I didn't want to have to shoot unless I needed to. The bow trembled in my left hand. The nock of the arrow, against my cheek, shook against my clammy skin. Connor's hot breath warmed my neck, and I knew he was just as afraid as I was.

But the scraping sounds continued, and soon, they began to fade. The ant was moving on. We hadn't been discovered, after all.

We waited for nearly a minute, until we heard no sounds. Finally, Connor spoke.

"Do you think he's gone?"

"Oh, I'm sure he's not gone for long," I said. "Besides, we have no idea how many ants there are. There could be dozens. Maybe hundreds."

"Or even thousands," Connor said.

I shuddered. Connor might be right. There was no telling how many giant ants were crawling around within the earth.

"Okay," I said, trying to sound brave. "We've got a job to do. We've got to find Annie, and we've got to get out of here."

I didn't say anything about the possibility of being too late to rescue our friend. I didn't want to think about it, and I certainly didn't want to say it out loud.

"Then, let's go," Connor said. He clicked on the flashlight, and the bright beam lit up the tunnel in front of us. I squinted in the harsh light, as my eyes had become used to the dark when Connor shut off the flashlight. Now, my eyes had to adjust to the light all over again.

We took a few steps forward, and once again, we were at the place where the tunnel branched off to the left and to the right.

"Let's go that way," I said, pointing to the right.

"That's where the ant came from. We might as well head in that direction and look for Annie."

Connor said nothing. He aimed the flashlight ahead of us. Roots dangled like thin snakes from above, long and wiry and crooked, casting wiry shadows in the murky gloom.

Connor spoke. "We have to be careful not to—"

He cut his sentence short when we heard a sound.

A gasp.

A sniffle.

A soft cry.

"That's Annie!" I said. "I know it is! Come on!"

We rushed forward. Connor stayed right beside me, and we followed the beam as it gave us light to see in the tunnel. We followed it as it zigzagged to the left and to the right, back and forth. All the while, I held out my bow, ready to pull back the arrow, raise it to my cheek, and let it fly. Connor carried the shovel at his side like a spear, ready to use it to defend himself.

"Annie!" I said, nearly shouting. "Annie! Can you hear us?"

"Scooter?" Annie replied, and I was relieved to hear her voice so close. Although we couldn't see her, she didn't sound far away at all.

"It's me!" I said. "Me and Connor! Where are you?"

"I'm right here!" Annie said. "I think I can see your light!"

Connor and I surged forward, bounding through the tunnel, ignoring the wiry roots that licked at our heads and shoulders.

Suddenly, Annie came into view. She was on the ground, curled into a ball, leaning against the side of the tunnel. Energized at the sight of our friend, Connor and I surged forward, dropping to our knees in front of Annie. I placed my bow and arrow off to the side.

"I can't believe we found you!" I said.

"I can't believe you did, either," Annie replied. She had been crying, and her cheeks were still wet. Now, she reached up with the ball of her fist and wiped the remnants of her tears away. Then, she rolled to her knees and got to her feet.

"Let's get out of here!" she said. "Let's get out of here, right now. Before those things come back."

"Are you hurt?" I asked.

"Just some scratches and scrapes," she replied.

"It could've been a lot worse."

Annie was lucky. Connor and I had been lucky, too. The three of us were now together, and we hadn't been harmed.

But we still had to get out, and that was a task that was going to be a lot harder than we could have ever imagined.

11

"Okay," I said. "Here's what we're going to do. Connor, stay right next to me and keep the light aimed ahead of us. Annie, you stay right behind me and Connor. The tunnel is pretty narrow, but at least it's big enough for us to stand up."

"What if one of those ants comes after us?" Annie asked.

"I'll be ready with my bow and arrow," I replied.

"And I've got a shovel," Connor said, making a spearing gesture with the garden tool.

"Cool," I said. "Ready?"

"No," Annie said. "What I meant was, what if an ant comes up behind us? You're in the front with a bow and arrow, and Connor has a shovel. I don't have anything."

I hadn't thought of that. If Annie was behind us and an ant attacked from the flank, she would have no way to protect herself.

Then, I remembered what I had in my back pocket.

"Here," I said, pulling out the can of insect spray. "Keep this ready. It's insect killer. If an ant comes up behind you, spray it."

"Will it work?" Annie asked, rolling the canister in her hands.

"Well," I said, "it says that it's insect killer. I would imagine that it kills bugs."

"Giant bugs?" Annie asked.

I shrugged. I wasn't sure if it would work on giant ants.

"Guys," Connor interjected, "let's stop wasting our time talking about this and get out of here."

Connor was right. We were wasting valuable seconds, time that we really needed to get out of the ground. Every second we spent in the tunnel was one second closer to danger.

"Let's move," I said.

Without another word, I turned around and started out. Connor huddled next to me, carrying the shovel in his right hand and the flashlight in his left. The beam illuminated the tunnel in front of me, and the dangling roots caused shadows to weave back and forth as we made our way through the earth.

"The good thing is," Connor said as we walked, "we don't have to worry about getting lost. All we have to do is find where the tunnel turned off to the left. That's the way out."

"And let's hope that's our only worry," I said. "Annie, are you doing okay?"

From behind me, Annie spoke. "Yeah," she said. "But I'll be doing a lot better when we get out of here."

With great relief, we soon came to the part of the tunnel that led out. One tunnel turned to the left, which would lead outside; in front of us, it continued on, deeper into the earth.

"Almost there," I said.

But just as I turned, I realized that our exit was going to be a little trickier than I thought. Ahead of us, I heard a noise, and there was only one thing it could be: a giant ant. Although I couldn't see it yet, I knew that it was not only blocking our way out . . . but it was coming toward us.

12

"Okay," I said quietly, trying to remain calm and hide my fear. "Stop. I think one of those things is coming. Back up."

I heard Annie gasp, but she began to move backward. Connor and I stepped back, and once again, we found ourselves at a crossroads of sorts, a 'T' in the tunnel. In front of us was the way out, but it was blocked by an ant. To the left of us was the direction we'd just come from, where we'd rescued Annie. To the right of us was the tunnel where Connor and I had hidden momentarily while an ant crawled by us. We had no idea where it went, and we didn't want to find out.

But being that we had good luck there before, I decided to head in that direction again . . . at least for the time being, to see if we could hide from the ant like we'd done before.

"This way!" I hissed and headed down the tunnel. "Stay close, and let's see if we can find another place to hide."

"Maybe this leads to another way out," Connor suggested.

"Maybe so," I said. "But then again, maybe it's just a larger part of a big maze. We can't go too far, especially if we come across more tunnels that split off to the sides. It'll be easy to lose our way and get lost. Then, we might never get out of here."

"Or we'll wind up getting eaten," Annie said.

"Aren't you the hopeful one," Connor said snidely.

"Hey," Annie snapped, "you weren't the one who got kidnapped. You weren't the one who got picked up and taken away by one of those things. I thought I was going to be lunch. When that thing put me down and crawled away, it was my only chance to escape. But it was so dark, and I couldn't see anything. I kept bumping into the walls. When I heard a noise, I thought it was one of those ants coming after me again, so I curled into a ball and hoped it would leave me alone. But it turned out to be you guys."

"You're lucky we came along when we did," Connor said. "You're lucky that—"

"Enough, guys," I said. "You're being too loud."

I stopped to listen, and Connor bumped into me. Annie bumped into Connor, and the three of us paused, listening.

Behind us, we heard continuous crawling sounds. However, it didn't sound like they were getting closer. It sounded like the ants were crawling in and out of the tunnel. They must have been following the tunnel to the right, heading away from us.

"Connor, you might be right," I said. "There might be another way out. Let's keep going this way, and see if we can find it. We'll have to be careful not to take any other side tunnels, if we happen to come across any. Otherwise, we'll get lost."

We continued making our way through the tunnel slowly, taking careful steps.

Suddenly, up ahead, the tunnel changed

dramatically. We discovered what appeared to be a brick wall, but the cement appeared to have been chipped away by a sledge hammer.

Or eaten away by something with sharp teeth and claws, I thought.

I stopped.

"Connor, give me the flashlight," I said. Holding my bow and arrow in my left hand, I took the flashlight in my right.

"What is it?" Annie asked. She had leaned in closer, and she and Connor were on either side of my shoulders.

"I don't know," I said. "It's some sort of wall with a hole in it."

Carefully, I knelt down and shined the light through the hole. The beam stretched out into darkness, reflecting a flat, cement floor in a big room.

But as I moved the beam back and forth, side to side, it illuminated other things.

Strange things. *Big* things.

And as I realized what they were, as I began to understand the horrifying scene before us, I realized that we were in deeper trouble than I could have ever imagined.

13

Connor sensed my fear and terror. His left hand was on my shoulder, and I could feel him tensing up.

"What is it?" he asked. "What do you see?"

I had a hard time answering him, because I wasn't sure what I was seeing myself. Oh, I *knew* what I was seeing, I just didn't believe it.

"Shhhh," I replied, in a voice just above a whisper. *"Giant ants. There must be twenty or thirty of them. I think it's their nest."*

Connor and Annie leaned in, poking their heads

over my shoulders. Slowly, I swept the beam around the great room.

Giant ants lay side-by-side, frozen and unmoving. They were in perfect rows, next to each other, like an army battalion waiting for orders.

Annie covered her mouth to stifle a gasp.

"How many of them are there?" Connor asked.

I shook my head. *"I haven't counted,"* I replied. *"And it doesn't really matter."*

"Are they sleeping?" Annie asked.

"I think so," I answered. *"Otherwise, they would be coming after us right now."*

Now, we were really in a bind. We'd come this way because there were ants behind us in the other direction. Now, we'd reached a dead end of sorts. We couldn't go forward because of the ants' nest. One little noise might awaken them.

"Looks like we have to go back," Connor said. "Because there's no way I'm going into that room."

"Me, neither," Annie said.

They were right. We had no other choice. We would have to go back the way we came and hope that the ants in the tunnel were gone.

"I really wish I would've stayed home," I said

quietly. "I wish I would've stayed home and maybe played Frisbee with Bo."

"Wishing isn't going to do anything," Connor said. "That's what my cousin always says. He says 'stop wishing and start doing.'"

"Okay," I said. "Let's stop wishing and go back."

The three of us were cramped together in the tunnel, and I needed to squeeze by Connor and Annie while being careful with the bow and arrow. I handed the flashlight back to Connor and told him to shine the beam in front of us.

Once again, we set out. Connor was next to me with the flashlight and the shovel, and Annie remained behind us.

"You still got that insect killer?" I asked her.

"Yeah," she said, holding it up.

We hustled through the tunnel. Soon, we came to the 'T.' The tunnel turned to the right, which was our way out, and straight ahead, which went farther into the earth.

And it was with great relief that we didn't see or hear any sign of the giant ants.

I turned and walked as fast as I could, holding my bow with my left hand, the arrow nock in my right, ready to defend us. Every step we took, every second that passed, I grew more excited. We were going to make it out.

Ahead of us, I glimpsed a faint light.

"We're almost out!" I said. "I can see daylight!"

Daylight gave us hope and a burst of energy. We moved even faster through the tunnel. In moments, we had scrambled out of the hole and exploded into the daylight . . . where just a few feet away, an enormous, giant ant was waiting to ambush us!

14

Without a moment's hesitation, I drew the arrow back, held the nock against my cheek, and let it fly. I didn't wait for the ant to attack, I didn't wait for him to charge us. I simply drew the arrow back and let it go.

The arrow hit the ant square in the head, and the effect was shocking. The creature slumped to the ground, collapsing on all six of its legs.

Behind me, Connor and Annie had emerged from the hole. They stood on either side of me, shocked.

The ant started moving. Its leg started quivering

and shaking, and its head started to roll back and forth.

"Shoot him again!" Connor exclaimed.

I pulled another arrow from the quiver and let it fly. It hit the insect in the back and stuck. Then, I shot another arrow, and another. The creature kept moving. I drew my last arrow, aimed for the ant's head, and let it fly. It buried itself into the exoskeleton next to the first arrow.

By then, the ant had succeeded in getting to its feet, but the last arrow caused it to fall again. Still, I hadn't killed it. I'd shot it with five arrows, but that still wasn't enough.

Annie stepped forward and held out the can of insect killer I had given her.

"Try this!" she said.

I grabbed the canister, took a few steps toward the ant, and began to spray. A gray mist coated the ant's head and a few of its legs, but it had no effect. Frustrated, I tossed the can aside and leapt back.

Connor stepped up and raised the shovel over his head like a spear. "I'll get him!" he said.

I shook my head. "Save it," I said. "Right now, let's get out of here before that thing comes to his senses and charges us!"

I tossed my bow to the ground. Without any arrows, it was worthless to me, and I didn't want to have the burden of carrying it as we raced home.

Home.

That's all I could think about. Once we got home, once we got inside, we would be safe. Maybe Mom had returned. If not, I would try to call her again. Maybe Mrs. Simms was home. Maybe we could call the police again and try to get them to believe us.

Although the arrows were still protruding out of its head and body, the giant insect was slowly getting to its feet. The arrows hadn't killed it, but they had slowed it down . . . and probably had made it mad. I wanted to get away from it as fast as I could.

The three of us darted around the ant and began sprinting through the field.

"You shot that thing five times, and it's still alive!" Annie shouted as she ran.

"But I think the arrows slowed him down!" I shouted back. "All we need to do is make it to my house. If we can do that, we'll be safe!"

Still, I had another fear.

What if there were more ants on the trail? What

if we encountered more of the bloodthirsty insects on our way back to my house?

We would have to worry about that when the time came.

We reached the trail and flew through the woods. Branches whipped past in a blur. Our feet drummed the hard-packed trail. We skirted around swamps, over small hills, and leapt over logs and brush. My eyes darted from side to side, then to the trail in front of us, and even into the trees above. I was searching for more ants, preparing for another ambush.

Finally, I saw the white metal shed at the back of our house. We'd made it. We'd made it home.

Almost.

At the edge of the forest, where the trees ended and our yard began, I stopped.

An electrical blanket of horror wrapped around my body, squeezing every muscle. Although I was tired from running and my lungs were heaving, I couldn't breathe.

"Oh, no," Annie gasped. She made another noise, and I thought she was going to puke. Instead, she dropped to her knees. Her hands flew up and covered her face.

"This can't be happening," she cried. "This isn't real! None of this can be real!"

She was right . . . but she was wrong. None of this *should* be happening. None of this *should* be real.

But it was.

The three of us could only stare.

Giant ants were crawling all over our house!

15

Not only were ants crawling over the house, but they seemed to be everywhere: we saw a couple climbing through the trees, one on the white metal shed, and one in the backyard near our picnic table. We counted seven, and there were probably more.

But so far, it didn't appear that they had spotted us.

Yet.

"Okay," I said very quietly. "I don't think any of them have seen us. Let's back up, very slowly, and hide in the woods. Don't move fast, don't do anything that might attract their attention. Connor, give me the flashlight, and be ready with the shovel."

Then, very slowly, Annie got to her feet. Connor handed me the flashlight, and the three of us stepped backward. We moved cautiously, as if our very lives depended on it.

And, as a matter of fact, our lives *did* depend on it. We'd been lucky that none of the ants had spotted us; otherwise, I'm sure they would have attacked. Now, we had a chance. It didn't mean we were safe, but for the moment, they hadn't spotted us.

"Crouch down in those bushes!" I hissed. *"Remember: move slowly!"*

Annie crouched down behind the bush, followed by Connor, who carefully clutched the shovel with both hands. Finally, I hunkered down next to my two friends. Concealed by the vegetation, we peered through the leaves and branches, watching the ants. Two of them were climbing on the roof of our house. One was scaling a wall, and there were two ants in nearby trees. The ant that had been on the metal shed was making his way across the backyard. He climbed over the picnic table, onto the porch, and began climbing up the wall to the roof.

"This is crazy!" Connor whispered.

"Look on the bright side," Annie said. *"If the teacher asks you to write something about what you did on summer break, you'll have a great story."*

I almost laughed out loud. Annie usually doesn't kid around like that, so it seemed even funnier coming from her.

"Yeah," Connor said, "that is, if we live long enough to go to school again."

"Somehow," I said, "we've got to get in the house. We'll be safe there."

"But those things are crawling all over the place," Connor said.

"Yeah, but they haven't spotted us," I replied. "If we stay here, hidden in these bushes and out of sight, we can wait. We can wait for a chance."

"A chance for what?" Annie asked.

"We wait until the ants are gone," I replied, "or at least until they move away from my house. It'll only take us a few seconds to get to the back door. If we can make it that far and inside, we're home free."

And so, we waited. We watched as the giant ants crawled around. They seemed to be in no hurry, and I had no idea what they were looking for, or if they were looking for anything in particular. They just seemed to be ambling about, doing nothing. They didn't pick up anything; they didn't chew on anything.

And, after a few minutes, the ants began to fan out. One of them wandered over to Mrs. Simms' house, followed by another. The two ants that had been in the trees crawled down, but we couldn't see where they went.

"What do you think?" I asked Connor and Annie. "Are you guys ready?"

Connor looked at the two ants in the neighboring yard.

"Do you think we can make it to your back door in time?" he asked.

In my mind, I tried to calculate how fast the ants could move, how much ground they could cover once they spotted us. I remembered how fast they had chased us through the woods. We had been able to stay away from them and keep a good distance ahead. Yes, they were fast, but I thought we would be faster.

I nodded my head. "I think we have a good chance," I said. "In fact, I think it's the best chance that we have. It will take us less than ten seconds to get to the back door. I'll go first, and you guys follow right behind me. Last one in, slam the door, and I'll throw the deadbolt."

I had been kneeling, but I slowly got to my feet while still crouching down. Connor and Annie did the same.

"Ready?"

Wordlessly, Connor and Annie affirmed by nodding their heads.

"Whatever you do, don't stop," I said. "Don't stop, and for crying out loud, don't trip and fall."

I took a breath, then exhaled. Then, I took another deep breath . . . and sprang.

My tennis shoes pounded the ground as I emerged from the forest. Although I didn't turn around to see, I could hear Connor and Annie right behind me, their shoes pummeling the earth.

I shot a glance into Mrs. Simms' yard. The two ants were looking the other way. They hadn't seen us. There were no other ants in sight.

Halfway there.

We approached the white metal shed, skirting around the right side of it.

Five more seconds. In five seconds, we'd be at

the back door. We were going to make it.

Unfortunately, we'd made a tragic mistake. We thought all of the ants had moved away, far enough for us to have enough time to get to the house.

Not so.

On the other side of the white metal shed, an ant had been waiting. Oh, he probably wasn't waiting for us, as he probably didn't know we were there.

Problem was, we didn't know that he was there, either, because he'd been concealed on the other side of the shed.

Suddenly, we were just a few feet from him, and with one quick motion, he was in front of us, blocking our way to the back door.

16

I was running so fast that I almost ran right into the ant. It was only at the last second that I was able to dart to the right, but even then, I tripped over my own feet and nearly fell. Annie leapt to the left of the insect and ran around it, continuing toward the back door.

Connor stopped. He wielded the shovel like a weapon before him.

"Go!" he said to me. "Get to your house! I'll fend him off!"

"Are you nuts?!?!" I said.

"Just go!" Connor insisted.

It was one of the bravest things I think I'd ever seen my friend do. He was willing to stand up to this gigantic creature, all by himself, with only a shovel to defend himself.

But I wasn't going to let him fight the beast alone. While the insect was focused on Connor, I took a few steps back, wielding the flashlight over my shoulder like a club.

"Just go!" Connor insisted again.

"I'm not going without you," I said. "Maybe I can create a distraction, and he'll—"

It was at that moment that the ant lunged at Connor. However, instead of leaping away or trying to step aside, Connor surged forward with the shovel. His intention was to spear the insect, but the ant was much faster. It grabbed the long garden tool with its two front legs and yanked it out of Connor's hands.

Connor was so shocked that he just stood there for a moment, his mouth hanging open like a dead fish.

The ant snapped the shovel into two pieces as easily as I would have broken a toothpick with my fingers.

Then, the insect lunged at Connor.

Without waiting another second, I threw the flashlight as hard as I could. It sailed through the air like a black metal pipe, tumbling end over end. In the moment before the ant grasped Connor, the flashlight struck the insect's head. It bounced off and tumbled to the ground. The beast was momentarily distracted, and turned.

As if suddenly awakening from a bad dream, Connor's eyes widened. He saw his opportunity for escape and darted to the left of the ant, racing around it and heading toward the back door where Annie waited for him.

"Hurry, Connor, hurry!" Annie urged.

I didn't waste any more time, either. I raced to the house, and in six long strides, I was bounding over the porch and through the open door. Annie slammed it shut. I grabbed the deadbolt and slammed it to the locked position. Then, I bent down and put my hands on my knees, still standing, but leaning over and gasping for breath.

"We . . . we made it," I heaved. "I can't believe it, but we made it."

"I didn't even see that thing behind the white shed," Connor said.

"I'm really glad you had that shovel," said Annie. "That saved your life."

"Scooter saved my life," Connor said, pointing at me. "If he hadn't had that flashlight, I wouldn't have made it."

I stood up straight, took a deep breath, and spoke. "Now, we can try calling for help again. I'll call the police one more time and see if they'll believe us. Annie, go look out the window and see if Mrs. Simms' car is in her driveway. Connor, go to the garage and see if there's anything else we can use to fight off those things."

"But we made it to the house," Connor said. "We're safe in here."

"Yeah, but just in case," I said.

I hustled into the kitchen and reached for the phone. While I was picking it up, I glanced out the living room window.

I froze.

"No!" I shouted. *"No! No! We have to stop them!"*

My shouts brought Connor into the kitchen, and Annie came running.

"What?" Annie asked. "What's wrong, Scooter?"

I pointed out the window.

Outside, by our mailbox, were two enormous ants. One was black, and one was dark brown with darker markings like a snake.

But that wasn't the horrifying part.

What scared me so much was that both of the ants were attacking Bo!

17

The sight of my friend Bo, the stray yellow Labrador, being attacked by not one but two giant ants was almost too much to bear. After all: Bo was a friend to everyone. He didn't have a mean bone in his body. He considered everyone his pal.

But these ants didn't consider Bo their friend. By the looks of it, they thought he was lunch.

There was no time to grab anything to defend myself. In looking back, I probably should've grabbed something—anything—to use as a weapon. But I could only focus on Bo. He was barking like mad, scared and confused. One of the ants came at him, and the dog backed away. When he did, the other ant came up from behind. Bo was surrounded. It wasn't a fair fight.

I burst out the front door and down the porch.

"Bo!" I shouted "Bo! Here, boy!"

Bo turned and saw me, but he was distracted by the black ant. The creature lunged at him and reached out with one of its front legs, striking the dog in the chest. Bo yelped in pain, fell over, but quickly got to his feet. If I was going to save him, I was going to have to do something, and fast.

"Scooter!" Connor called out. I turned to see him and Annie in the front doorway, huddled together, watching me.

"I've got to save Bo!" I yelled.

"You're going to get killed!" Annie shouted.

And the really strange thing? Annie was right. I might get killed. But at that moment, I didn't care. I was so worried about Bo that I wasn't concerned about myself. I know that might seem silly, but that's just the kind of friend Bo was. He was just as good of a friend as Connor and Annie. I would've done the same for each one of them.

And they would do the same for me.

So, instead of standing in the doorway watching helplessly, Connor and Annie came to my aid. They bounded across the porch, down the steps, and into the yard to where I stood.

"Get back in the house!" I said.

"Not without you," Connor said.

"Yeah, and Bo, too," said Annie. "He's our friend, too, you know."

A sense of pride swelled inside of me. I was so grateful to have such terrific friends who cared not only about me, but about the defenseless stray dog.

We tried calling him, but Bo was too focused on the charging ants. It was as if the insects were only playing with him. For the time being, the dog was holding his ground, but I knew it was only going to be a matter of time before the ants wore him out. When that happened, one of the bugs would get the best of him. Then, my furry friend would be done for.

I've got to think of a way to get the ants away from him, I thought. *Or get Bo away from the ants.*

I suddenly thought of something.

"Bo!" I yelled. "Treat!"

The dog stopped barking and spun, looking at me. He raised his ears and cocked his head.

"That's right, boy!" I said as sweetly as I could. "I have a tasty treat for you! Come and get it! Treat! Treat!"

It was the word Bo could never resist. He knew he was in for something good when I told him I had a treat.

Bo bounded toward me. It was as if the ants no longer existed. He forgot all about them. He charged toward me, his pink tongue flapping from side to side, his tail wagging. Ants no longer mattered. To Bo, the only thing that mattered was filling his belly with a tasty morsel.

"That's it, Bo!" Annie shouted. "Come on, Bo!"

Even before he reached us, we began running back to the house. At the end of the driveway, the two ants had figured out what had happened. Their prey had slipped away, and they were now scrambling toward us.

And they looked angrier than ever.

Up the stairs and over the porch we went, sailing through the doorway. Bo was last, and when he came through, I slammed the door and locked it.

"We made it!" Connor said. "We saved Bo!"

Without wasting any time, I went into the

kitchen. In the refrigerator, I found some leftover steak. If there was any food that Bo absolutely loved, it was meat. I gave him a big hunk, and he wolfed it down.

"Good boy," I said, and he happily wagged his tail as he chewed. "You were almost lunch for those ugly things." I patted him on the head. "You sure are one brave dog."

Outside, there was no sign of the two ants. They'd vanished.

"Where did they go?" Annie asked.

"I don't know, and I don't care," I said. "All I care about is that we're inside, and we're safe. Bo is safe, too. Now, we can call for help."

I was thankful that our ordeal was about to come to an end. We were safe inside our house, and I knew that soon, help would come. If we couldn't get the police to believe us, Mom would. She would believe us, for sure. Especially when she saw the giant ants for herself!

But it's funny how things just don't work out the way you plan them. Sometimes, no matter how hard you try, nothing goes the way you want it to. There's always a lesson to be learned; there's always one more hurdle you have to get over, even when you think you've come to the end of the race . . . and we were about to find that out the hard way.

18

I snapped up the wireless phone from the kitchen counter and turned it on. However, before I pressed the numbers, I quickly noticed something. I frowned.

"What?" Connor asked. "What is it?"

"There's no dial tone," I said. "This phone has a landline, so there should be a dial tone when you turn it on. There's not."

I held the receiver to my ear and listened.

Silence.

"I wonder if the ants chewed through the phone lines on the outside of the house," I said.

"Must be some pretty smart ants," Connor said.

"Don't you have another phone?" Annie asked.

I shook my head. "Nope," I replied. "Mom and Dad say I'm not old enough for one yet."

"That's awful," Annie said.

"Where's *your* phone?" Connor asked Annie.

Annie's eyes widened, and she pursed her lips in embarrassment. "My parents won't let me have one, either," she said sheepishly.

"Okay, okay," I said. "Don't worry. Just because we don't have a phone doesn't mean it's the end of the world. All we have to do is wait for my mom to come home."

"But what if the ants attack her when she gets out of the car?" Connor asked.

I shook my head. "We have an electric garage door opener," I said. "Mom always drives the car into the garage and closes the door behind her. As long as ants don't follow her into the garage, she'll be fine."

At that moment, I spotted a movement out the dining room window.

"It's a car!" Connor said.

"It's your mom!" said Annie.

Connor was right, but Annie wasn't. It was a

car, all right. But it wasn't my mom. It was Mrs. Simms, our neighbor. We watched as her car traveled along the road in front of our house and turned into her driveway.

"Wait a minute!" Connor said. "Mrs. Simms doesn't have a garage! That means she's going to get out of her car!"

Annie's eyes widened. "She doesn't know anything about the ants!" she said. "Mrs. Simms is going to be a sitting duck!"

We raced to the living room window. Mrs. Simms was parking her car in front of her house.

The driver's side door opened.

I raced to the front door, unlocked it, and threw it open.

"Mrs. Simms!" I shouted. "Mrs. Simms! Get back in your car! Giant ants are crawling all over the place!"

Mrs. Simms, alerted by my shouts, turned. She smiled and waved, but didn't understand what I had said.

Connor and Annie joined me in the doorway.

"Scooter is right!" Connor shouted. "There are giant bugs all over the place!"

In response, Mrs. Simms only rolled her eyes

and laughed. Clearly, she understood what we were saying. But, like the police dispatcher, Mrs. Simms didn't believe us.

But she was about to.

On the roof of her house, a giant ant came into view. Then, another.

Annie pointed. "Look up there!" she shouted. "On the roof! On the roof!"

Mrs. Simms had retrieved a bag of groceries from her front seat. Casually, she looked up to see what Annie was pointing at.

The brown bag of groceries suddenly fell from her arms and crashed to the ground. The paper tore open, and the contents of the bag spilled out all over the gravel driveway. Mrs. Simms shrieked and covered her mouth with one hand.

"Well," Connor said, "I think she believes us now."

Suddenly, something hit my leg with such force that it nearly knocked me down. It hit Connor, too, and he fell to the side, grasping Annie before he tumbled over.

"What—"

But before Connor could get the words out, we

both knew what had happened.

Bo had bolted between our legs and out the door. He sailed off the porch, into the yard, and bounded toward Mrs. Simms. He was going to save her!

Unfortunately, Bo never got that far. Unknown to him and to us, there was a huge ant in the bushes between our house and Mrs. Simms' house. Mrs. Simms couldn't see it, of course, and neither could we. And Bo certainly had no idea the insect was hiding there.

With one swift motion, the ant attacked, crawling out of the bushes with such speed that there was nothing we could do. Before I could shout to Bo, before I could even move, the giant ant was upon him. With one easy sweep of its front two legs, the huge freak snapped up the surprised dog. Bo let out a painful yelp, but it was too late to do anything. In a split second, the ant spun, turned, and took off into the woods, carrying my best friend with him.

19

Mrs. Simms stood in her driveway next to her car. One hand covered her mouth. Her eyes appeared abnormally large, the size of baseballs. At her feet, groceries—bananas, apples, bags of vegetables, canned goods—were splayed out all over the place. A box of ice cream had broken open, and the white cream was quickly melting, dripping onto the gravel driveway and forming a small puddle.

"What on Earth?!?!" Mrs. Simms shouted.

"Mrs. Simms!" I called out, pointing at the roof of her house. "Get inside! There are more of those things on your roof! Get inside!"

Mrs. Simms turned to look where I was pointing. Then, seeing the ants on her roof, she screamed again. She took off running toward her house, not bothering to close her car door or pick up her groceries. She threw open the front door, darted inside, and slammed the door behind her.

"Wow," Annie said. "That was close. At least she's safe."

Annie was right, and I was glad, too. Mrs. Simms was safe.

But Bo was gone. We'd saved him once, only to have him snapped up into the clutches of yet another horrifying giant ant.

Connor looked at me. He knew that I was crushed, but he also knew there was nothing we could do. It was far too dangerous to go after Bo now, especially since we had no idea how many ants we would be up against.

No, the only thing we could do was wait in our house. We would wait, wonder, and hope. Sooner or later, help would arrive.

Unfortunately, I couldn't help but think that it probably would be too late for Bo.

Then, Annie did something that was totally unexpected. She knew how sad I was over losing Bo. She reached out with both arms, wrapped them around me, and gave me a big, tight hug.

"He's going to be okay," she said as she drew back. "I know it. Bo is too smart. He's too brave. He'll get away. I know he will."

It was nice of her to say so, and I appreciated the thought and gesture. I managed to smile and nod, but that's all I could do.

"Annie's right," Connor chimed in. "Bo is a really smart dog. He'll figure it out. He'll get away, somehow."

I walked into the living room and looked out the window, hoping that just maybe I might see Bo coming back.

Nope.

I turned and looked at Mrs. Simms' house, and my spirits lifted. Mrs. Simms was standing in her open doorway with a phone to her ear! She was talking to someone!

"Guys!" I said excitedly, pointing. "Mrs. Simms is on her phone! The ants haven't chewed through her phone lines!"

Connor and Annie raced to my side, and they looked out the window.

"It looks like she's on her smart phone," I said, "so it wouldn't matter if the ants chewed through the lines."

"I'm sure she's on the phone with the police right now!" Connor said. "They have to believe her. She's an adult."

"It's only a matter of time, now," Annie said. "Finally, this whole thing is going to be over. Finally, we'll be able to—"

"Shhhh!" I hissed, interrupting Annie. "Did you hear that?"

The three of us were silent. At first, there was nothing to hear. And then:

A dog barking. It was far away, and it sounded like it was coming from the woods in back of the house, but it was a dog, I was certain.

And I knew something else.

"I'd know that bark anywhere!" I exclaimed excitedly. "That's Bo! I know it is!"

We raced through the living room, into the kitchen, and to the back door. I threw back the deadbolt, grasped the knob, and threw the door open.

At first, we didn't see anything. We could hear Bo barking in the woods, and we could hear the crashing of brush and the snapping of twigs and branches.

"He's coming this way!" Connor said. "He got away! I knew he would!"

Suddenly, Bo appeared, sailing out from a thick wall of branches. Leaves and tiny twigs were stuck to his dirty fur coat.

And he was being chased by an entire brigade of army ants . . . and they were right behind him!

20

I've never seen Bo so frightened in his life. Up until now, I'd always seen him happy. Sure, he was kind of mangy and dirty, but he was always happy. And he never seemed afraid. Bo was always so sweet and gentle, and people in the neighborhood always treated him kindly.

But this was a new experience for him. Now, he was up against bloodthirsty insects that wanted him dead . . . and probably wanted him for a meal. Or maybe they wanted to take him back to their nest to feed their queen.

For whatever reason, the ants wanted Bo, and they wanted him badly. They were in hot pursuit as they chased him across the yard, and every second brought the dog and the insects closer to the house, closer to the back door.

"There must be a dozen of those things!" Annie shrieked.

Connor grabbed the knob. "Close the door, close the door!" he wailed as he pushed, but I fought his efforts.

"Not until Bo gets inside!" I insisted.

"You're crazy!" Connor said. "The ants are right behind him!"

"We're not closing the door until Bo is inside, and that's all there is to it!" I said firmly. "Now . . . are you going to help me?"

"All right," Connor said. "Annie! Help us! It's going to take all three of us to keep the door closed if those ants try to break through."

Within seconds, Bo was bounding across the back porch. Behind him, a mountain of army ants followed. Most of them were a dark, reddish-brown, and some had yellow markings. Others had black blotches or brown rings. All of them looked horrifying.

All of them looked angry and mean.

Bo bounded through the doorway, and the three of us slammed the door shut.

We weren't quick enough.

One of the ants managed to get a leg through the opening, and we couldn't get the door closed. A spiny, bony claw, longer than my arm, wriggled and flung about. It had long pincers, like fingers, and one of them caught Connor's shirt sleeve and created a long tear.

"That thing just tore my shirt!" Connor screeched.

"You're lucky he didn't tear open your arm!" I said. "Keep pushing on the door! Don't let him get another leg through!"

The sounds the ants were making were maddening, like hundreds of fingernails on a chalkboard. We could hear them crawling along the wall outside, clawing their way up to the roof. Some of their legs smacked the windows, but so far, no glass had broken.

Finally, the ant trying to get inside withdrew his leg, and it was the chance we needed. The door slammed closed, and I slid the deadbolt into place.

We didn't shout in victory; there was no celebration, not even for a second. We were still in deep trouble, and we knew it. Ants were crawling all over the house, up the walls outside and onto the roof. I couldn't imagine what would've happened if one had made it inside. He would've torn us to shreds, for sure.

Bo, however, had returned to his usual, happy-go-lucky self. Moments ago, he had been frightened and more terrified than ever. Now, he acted as if it was all some sort of game. He stood in the kitchen, wagging his tail, looking at me, then Connor, then Annie, then back to me. He had completely forgotten that he had been chased by killer insects, that his life had been in danger.

I smiled and shook my head. "You crazy dog," I said as I opened up the refrigerator. Bo licked his chops because he knew something good was coming. And he was right: I gave him another piece of the meat we'd been saving. He wolfed it down in only a few quick chews.

All around the house, we could hear the sound of ants crawling everywhere. Their claws were scratching the wood siding and the roof. It was impossible to know how many there were. Besides:

something told me that I didn't *want* to know.

Then, we heard another sound, and it struck a chord of alarm in me. This wasn't the sound of scratching or scraping. It was the sound of chewing. It was the distinct sound of wood splintering and breaking . . . and it sounded like it was coming from my bedroom.

I raced down the hall. Connor and Annie followed me, and Bo brought up the rear.

Pushing open my bedroom door, I was stunned and horrified to see a hole in the wall near my bedroom window!

"Holy cow!" Connor shouted. "Scooter! Those things are chewing through your house! They're chewing through the wood!"

Bo started barking and growling, but I didn't pay any attention to him. Something inside of me had broken. Something inside of me had given up. After everything we had done to make it to the house, after everything we'd been through, we'd led ourselves into our own trap. We were surrounded by vicious, giant army ants . . . and they were going to chew their way through the house to get us.

21

"We have to get out of here," I said, and I was amazed at how calmly I spoke. On any other day, at any other time, if a giant ant would've been chewing through our house, I probably would've went running off right away, screaming my head off. However, we'd been through so much already that I knew I couldn't panic. A giant ant chewing through the wall of our house was only one more problem in a line of obstacles.

But it *was* a serious problem. As soon as the ant chewed a hole through the wall, he'd be able to get inside. Once one ant made it inside, the rest would follow. For a brief moment, I wondered why they didn't simply break a window. It would've been much easier to break a window and get inside, instead of chewing through an entire wall of paneling, wood, and wires.

"But where are we going to go, Scooter?" Annie asked. "We can't leave the house, because there are ants all over the place."

"Well, we can't stay here," I said. "Those things are coming after us. They're going to chew right through the walls of our house and get inside. Then, we'll be trapped."

"If we could only make it over to Mrs. Simms' house," Connor suggested. "Her house is made of bricks. The ants probably won't be able to chew through cement."

"But Connor," Annie pleaded, "like I said: those things are all over the place out there. How are we going to leave Scooter's house and get to Mrs. Simms' without being attacked and eaten?"

"Follow me," I said, and I led Connor, Annie, and Bo down the hallway to the living room. Outside, we saw an ant at the end of our driveway. He was eating the mailbox like it was a lollipop.

"Okay," I said. "There's one ant out there." Then, I pointed to a tree at the end of the street. "There's another one up there, and he's too far away to get to us. We know there's one chewing a hole in my bedroom wall. There are more on the roof." I looked over at Mrs. Simms' house. "There's only one on her roof," I said. "Mrs. Simms is still standing in her doorway, talking on her phone. If we all ran at the same time, and we ran fast, we could make it there before any ants got a hold of us."

"You're out of your mind," Annie said, shaking her head.

"No," Connor said, coming to my defense. "Scooter is right. We can do it. If we stick together and run fast, we can make it. Besides: we don't have any other choice. No one is here to help us yet, and we can't stand here and wait for those ants to chew a hole in the wall and get to us."

I hustled into the kitchen and opened the refrigerator. This drew Bo's attention, and he was at my heels in an instant, looking at me hopefully, wanting me to give him something to eat.

I pulled out yet another small piece of meat and held it up for the dog to see.

"You want this, buddy?" I asked. "You want a treat? All you have to do is follow us."

I carried the morsel in my fist and strode back to meet my friends by the front door. Bo obediently followed.

Annie, Connor, and I peered cautiously through the window to make sure there weren't any ants close by. Oh, I'm sure they were everywhere, but from what we could see, we had a clear shot from our front door to Mrs. Simms' front door. As long as she stayed where she was, she would see us coming. She would keep the door open for us, and we'd be able to get inside.

"Ready?" I asked.

Connor nodded. "I'm about as ready as—"

Connor's sentence was cut short by a crashing sound, the sound of splintering and exploding wood from my bedroom. I was sure that the ant had succeeded in chewing a hole in the wall big enough for him to get through. It would be only a matter of seconds before he was in the living room.

Nothing more was said. I didn't yell *'run!'* or *'go!'* I simply threw open the front door, and the three of us, followed by Bo, began running. I had estimated it would take about fifteen seconds to get to Mrs.

Simms' front door; it was about to become the longest fifteen seconds of my life.

22

At first, I thought our short sprint over to Mrs. Simms' was going to be a piece of cake. When we dashed over the porch and down the steps, I didn't see any ants besides the one by the mailbox and the one in the tree at the end of the street.

However, there were many more than I could have imagined.

Suddenly, two appeared on Mrs. Simms' roof. There were two more crawling on the side of our house that were out of our range of vision when we'd been at the front door. And from the scrambling and scraping sounds we heard, there were probably five or six more on the roof of our house.

Squeezing the cool, wet piece of meat in my right fist, I swung my arms in tandem with my legs, furiously pumping my limbs, racing across the lawn. I was dimly aware that Bo was right at my heels. For him, this was a game. This was just what he was doing to earn his treat. He had no idea the danger we were all facing.

Mrs. Simms saw us running toward her house. She was still holding the telephone to her ear, and her jaw dropped. She muttered something into the telephone and then lowered it. She pushed the door open farther and shouted, urging us on.

"Hurry, Scott! Hurry! Run faster!"

It sounded strange to hear my name. My friends, my teacher, even my parents hardly ever called me 'Scott.' Everybody called me Scooter or 'Scoot' for short. That is, of course, except for Mrs. Simms. She'd always called me by my given first name.

The ant that had been chewing on the mailbox tossed aside what was left of the mangled metal and wood and came after us. I wasn't too worried about him, because he was far enough away that I was sure we could outrun him.

The problem was going to come from the ants on our roof. Two of them dropped to the ground and landed on their rear legs like Olympic gymnasts. In seconds, we were surrounded.

Someone screamed, but I didn't know if it was Annie or Mrs. Simms. Bo, now fully alarmed, went into fighting mode. The hackles on his back stood up, and he began circling one of the ants, snapping and snarling, barking and growling. For such a friendly, loving dog, he sure could be protective and threatening. He didn't want anything to happen to us, his friends. Once again, he was risking his own life to save us.

Seeing Bo act with such bravery gave me a surge of confidence. Instinct took over. I didn't want to fight, because I knew it would be a losing battle. But somehow, we needed to create a diversion, we needed to do something to give us an avenue of escape. We needed to flee and take flight, not stand our ground and fight.

The problem was that we were defenseless. We hadn't had time to get anything to defend ourselves. Besides: how do you defend yourself against giant ants? My bow and arrow hadn't been of much use, and the shovel proved to be useless, as the ant had snapped it in two pieces. And the insect killer hadn't worked at all.

But Bo was really causing a stir, and he had the attention of both ants. The dog was taking turns barking and snarling at each of the insects, and the ants became completely focused on him. But the two bugs were still right in front of us, blocking our route to Mrs. Simms' house.

I squeezed the morsel of cold meat in my right hand. I held it up.

"Bo!" I shouted. "Treat!"

This took his attention away from the two ants. He stopped growling and snarling, gave me a goofy, silly look, and wagged his tail.

I knew I had only one or maybe two seconds, if I was lucky.

Drawing back my arm, I threw the piece of meat into Mrs. Simms' yard as hard as I could.

"There you go!" I yelled. "Go get it, Bo! Go get your treat!"

Bo watched the piece of pink meat fly through the air. Leaving the ants behind, he took off running after the treat. The two insects immediately took up chase . . . and that was all we needed. They weren't paying attention to us, and now Connor, Annie, and I had a straight shot at Mrs. Simms' front door.

"Go! Go! Go!" I shouted.

The plan worked perfectly. Not only did we make it to the door where Mrs. Simms held it open so we could get inside, but Bo had scooped up the treat in the yard without even stopping. While he ran toward us, he chewed the piece of meat. Once, he looked behind to see the ants in pursuit, but he never slowed down. He tore across the driveway, leapt onto the porch, and flew through the doorway. Mrs. Simms slammed the door closed with such force that the windows and pictures on the walls rattled.

We were safe, at least for the moment. I knew that Mrs. Simms had called for help, and I was sure that emergency services were on their way by now. Who would come? The police? Firemen? The National Guard? The Army? Maybe they would send a Navy Seal Team. Or maybe a force of exterminators specially trained to kill giant bugs.

I wasn't sure, and I really didn't care. I was just glad we were safe, that we were all together, with Bo.

No one had been hurt, and Connor had suffered only a torn shirt.

We'd been very, very lucky . . . but not for much longer.

23

As soon as the front door closed, Connor, Annie, and I began talking all at once. Mrs. Simms was overwhelmed, and she raised her hands and displayed her palms, urging us to calm down, to be quiet.

"One at a time, one at a time," she said.

"Did you find out what's going on?" I asked.

"Where did these ants come from?" asked Connor.

Before Mrs. Simms could answer, we were distracted by a crunching sound outside. The three of us followed our neighbor through her foyer, down the hall, and into her living room. Mrs. Simms has a huge picture window that looks out into her front yard. From there, we could see her car with the driver's side door open. We could see her groceries scattered all over the ground.

But we also saw ants. I counted five of them. One of them had crawled on top of her car and had leaned over with its head stretched down, peering into the driver's side through the open door. Another ant had picked up a bunch of bananas and was carefully inspecting the yellow fruit. I thought it was going to eat them all with one gulp, but instead, it tossed the bananas aside and picked up a large can of something. The insect inspected the item for a moment before discarding it like it had done with the bananas.

Meanwhile, Bo was having a wonderful time on his own. He ran around Mrs. Simms' house, sniffing everything, checking out the new smells.

"Bo, here," I said, but the dog just gave me a quick look, wagged his tail, and kept about his business of sniffing things around the house.

"I'm not sure if I can answer all of your questions," Mrs. Simms said. "I still don't understand what's going on myself. Are you children alone?"

We nodded. "My mom ran over to a friend's house to help her with her computer," I replied. "She should be back at any time."

Connor pointed at Annie. "She and I each live about a mile away from here. We just came over to visit Scooter."

"Have you been in your house all this time?" Mrs. Simms asked.

I shook my head and hiked my thumb over my shoulder. "Connor and I were back in the woods. We saw a couple of ants, and they came after us."

"I came looking for Connor and Scooter," Annie interjected, "but some ants kidnapped me."

"They took her into the ground," said Connor.

"I thought I was going to get eaten," Annie said.

"We followed the ants into their hole and saved Annie," I said.

"But is it just you three?" Mrs. Simms asked.

"Just us and Bo," I replied. "We're safe. But where did these things come from? How many of them are there?"

Mrs. Simms looked out the window at the giant ants in her yard.

"Well, I'm not sure exactly how many of them

there are," she said. "But they're definitely not what you think they are."

"You mean they're not ants?" Annie asked.

Mrs. Simms shook her head. "Yes and no," she said.

Connor and I looked at each other, confused.

"What do you mean?" I asked. "Are they ants?"

"Well, yes, they *are* ants," Mrs. Simms replied. "But they're not *insects.*"

Now, I was *really* confused. But when Mrs. Simms began explaining what they were, we understood what she meant. The mystery was solved. In an odd way, it made perfect sense. More sense than real, live, giant ants.

But the bad news for us was this: we were in far more danger than we had even imagined.

24

"What do you mean?" Annie asked. "How can they be ants, but not insects?"

"Simple," Mrs. Simms replied. "They're robots. Machines. They're top-secret robots designed by a computer company. Some sort of computer virus or malfunction has caused them to go crazy. They're trying to stop them right now, but until then, everyone is being told to stay in their houses."

"A lot of good that will do," I said, pointing to our house next door. By now, the ants had chewed several holes through the walls and were crawling in and out of our house. Mom and Dad were going to go bananas when they saw the damage.

"I don't know all the details," Mrs. Simms said. "The man on the phone told me to stay inside and keep my doors and windows closed. He said help is on the way."

Robots? I thought. *A computer malfunction? What is really going on here? How did things go this wrong? And why did somebody create something so dangerous in the first place?*

"How long are we going to have to wait?" Connor asked. "I've got to go home soon. Otherwise, my mom is going to be really worried."

"Mine, too," Annie said.

Mrs. Simms still had the phone in her left hand, and she held it up.

"You can use my phone to call your parents," Mrs. Simms said. "You can let them know you're all right. But for the time being, I think it's safest for you to stay right here. Tell your parents you're okay, but you can't leave just yet. If you want, I'll talk to them. I'm sure they'll understand that this is the safest place for all of you."

Mrs. Simms handed the phone to Connor, and

he called his mom and stepped to the other side of the living room to have his conversation. Annie, Mrs. Simms, and I stood by the window, looking outside, watching the ants as they crawled around.

"Now that you mention it," I said to Mrs. Simms, "they really do look like robots. They look like they're made out of some sort of metal."

"I'm not sure what they're made of," Mrs. Simms replied. "And I'm not sure if I want to find out. The only thing I want to do is stay indoors where it's safe. Thank you for warning me just in time. If you hadn't been there to alert me, I might not be alive right now."

Bo had finished his inspection of Mrs. Simms' house. He trotted up to her, nuzzling her hand. Mrs. Simms patted him on the head and scratched his ears.

"Are you still wandering around looking for a home?" she asked the dog.

"I keep asking my mom and dad if we can keep him," I said, "but they keep telling me no. I love him, and he's my best friend. I sure wish he could stay with us, because I worry about him."

Connor finished his conversation and handed the phone to Annie who, in turn, called her parents.

They wanted to talk to Mrs. Simms, so Annie handed the phone to her, and Mrs. Simms went into the kitchen to explain.

Annie, Connor, Bo, and I stood by the window.

"Just when you thought the day couldn't get any crazier," Connor said.

"I just hope help arrives soon," I said. "I hope they stop those things before somebody gets hurt."

"Maybe somebody's been hurt already," Annie said. "Maybe people have been killed, but we don't know it yet."

It was an awful thought. The three of us, and Bo, had been lucky, but maybe there were other people who hadn't been as fortunate. I'm sure we'd find out soon enough, because if someone had been hurt—or worse—I knew we'd hear about it on the news.

I turned to see if Mrs. Simms was off the phone. When she was done, I wanted to call my mom to let her know that I was okay. And I was going to tell her to not come home yet, that it was too dangerous.

And if she didn't believe me? Well, I would let her talk to Mrs. Simms. Mom would believe *her,* I was sure.

Then, there was an enormous crash. The entire

house shuddered and shook. Bo jumped and yelped.

We turned as the front door splintered and exploded inward . . . and two giant ants stood in the doorway!

25

Bo, snarling and barking, charged the ants like an enraged lion.

"Bo!" I shouted. *"No!"*

"Children!" Mrs. Simms shouted, stuffing her telephone into the front pocket of her jeans. *"Down the hall and into the bathroom!"* she shouted.

I didn't question anything. Connor, Annie, and I took off running. Again, I shouted at Bo.

"Bo! Come on! This way!"

Thankfully, Bo turned and left the two giant

ants. They were struggling to get through the doorway, but both of them were trying to get through at the same time, and they wouldn't fit.

That gave us the time we needed to get down the hall and into the bathroom. Connor was first, followed by Annie, then me, then Bo. Mrs. Simms followed us in and locked the door.

"Are you sure this is a good idea?" Connor asked, his breath heaving. "I mean, now we're trapped in a little, tiny room. If those ants can break down the front door, they can probably break down the bathroom door." He looked around, spotted a small window with a curtain over it, and pointed. "And that window's not big enough for us to crawl out if we need to escape."

Mrs. Simms reached up over the bathtub and grasped the curtain rod.

"Well," she said. "The bathroom door is pretty solid. Plus, we might be able to use this."

She yanked down the curtain rod and stripped the curtain from it, displaying a long, metal pipe. She placed one end against the wall behind us, and then the other end against the bathroom door.

"It might not stop them for long," Mrs. Simms

said, "but it might hold them off long enough for help to arrive. They should be here any minute."

"But what if they don't get here in time?" Annie replied.

"We'll just have to hope that they do," Mrs. Simms said.

I didn't like the sound of that. We were pretty much helpless, and the only thing that stood between us and death was a bathroom door and a metal pipe.

None of us said anything for the next few moments. Instead, we listened. Outside, we could hear the ants scrambling over the walls and the roof. And we could hear ants crashing through the inside of the house, knocking over things, breaking things.

I heard the sound of lapping water and turned to look down. Bo was drinking water out of the toilet!

"Bo!" I said. "No! That's not for drinking!"

Annie laughed, and that got Connor laughing. Mrs. Simms started chuckling, and soon all of us were laughing. Despite everything going on around us, despite the danger we were in, we were still able to find something funny in the situation.

Bo looked at me sheepishly and wagged his tail. "You're a good boy," I said as I patted his head. He licked my hand and sat.

The phone in Mrs. Simms' pocket chirped, and she dug it out and raised it to her ear.

"Hello?" she said. There was a pause, and she looked at me. Then, she looked at the floor. Her eyes lit up, she smiled, and she formed a thumbs-up sign with her other hand. "That's great news!" she said. "I'm so glad that this is going to be over soon." She paused, then continued. "Yes," she said, "the children are with me, and we're all safe. We've barricaded ourselves in the bathroom. We even have a stray dog with us." Mrs. Simms reached down and patted Bo's head, and the dog thumped his tail happily. "Oh, don't worry," Mrs. Simms continued, "we aren't going anywhere."

She lowered the phone and returned it to her pocket.

"That was the police," she said. "They're going to be here at any moment, along with the people from the computer company, the ones who made the creatures. They'll know what to do."

"I hope so," Annie said.

There was a scratch on the bathroom door.

Bo started growling.

There was another scratch.

I hope that metal curtain rod holds, I thought. *I hope that thing is strong enough to keep—*

Suddenly, the bathroom door crumbled like paper, and we were face to face with the biggest, meanest-looking beast I had ever seen in my life.

And we were trapped. There was nowhere we could go.

26

The four of us backed into the bathroom as far as we could, stepping into the bathtub and pressing against the wall. Bo stood his ground, snarling and snapping and barking at the furious insect. Annie was screaming, and so was Mrs. Simms.

The ant tried to push his way inside the bathroom, but he was so big, he almost didn't fit.

Almost.

He was big, but he was able to wriggle his legs free, and they were slashing wildly in front of us, crisscrossing dangerously, only inches from our faces.

Mrs. Simms had told us that they were robots, and if that was the case, they were the most dangerous robots in the world. I couldn't imagine why anyone would make a machine-creature like this. What would its purpose be? I mean, it would be great to have one as a Halloween decoration in the yard during October, as it would probably scare a lot of people. That would be fun.

But an actual ant-like robot that attacked people? That's just crazy.

Mrs. Simms and Annie were still screaming. Connor was yelling something, but I didn't know what he was saying. Bo was barking and snarling, snapping at the creature's legs as it tried to squeeze into the bathroom.

I looked down and saw the metal curtain rod. It hadn't broken or bent, but had fallen to the floor. One end was propped up on the ledge of the bathtub.

I quickly grabbed it and held it out in front of me. The curtain rod was longer than the creature's legs, so I was actually able to poke him in the head and chest without him touching me. In fact, I pushed so hard that I succeeded in forcing him backward.

"Connor!" I shouted. *"Grab the curtain rod and*

help me! Push with me! We can push him back out into the hall!"

Connor stepped next to me and grabbed the curtain rod. Together, we poked and pushed and prodded at the black beast. All the while, Bo kept growling and snapping, barking like crazy, the hair on his back standing straight up.

"It's working!" Annie cried. "You're fighting him off!"

While the ant-robot backed up, Connor and I inched forward, pushing the creature farther and farther into the hall. I had no idea what we were going to do if we were able to push the thing back to the living room. Maybe that would give us enough time to get into another room and close the door. Sure, the ant might break through that door, too, but it might buy us some time. I didn't know how long it was going to take for the police to get there, but I knew that every second counted.

Besides: I wasn't just going to stand there in the bathroom and let that thing tear us to pieces or carry us away.

Then, the unthinkable happened.

Connor and I tried to hit the creature in the

upper chest, but we missed and the curtain rod went over his shoulder. This caught me off guard, and I stumbled forward, which caused me to let go of the curtain rod.

The ant seized me with one of his powerful legs and pulled me to him.

I screamed bloody murder. Behind me, Bo went absolutely bananas. He barked and growled louder than ever, and I could hear his teeth snapping and grinding at the insect's legs.

"Scooter!" Connor shouted.

I was being held so tightly by the ant that I couldn't shout; I couldn't yell anything back.

Connor still had hold of the curtain rod, and he gave the insect one hard push. For a moment, the creature let go of me. However, instead of falling to the ground, I decided to try something else. I knew it was crazy, I knew it might be the end of me, but it was the only thing I could think of.

Using both of my arms, I wrapped them around the giant creature's beach ball-sized head. I pulled myself over his shoulders, and within a split second, I was on his back, one leg on either side of him, the way you'd ride a horse. The creature used his legs to try to grab me, but none of them would reach behind him that far.

Connor kept poking at the creature, and it continued retreating into the hall. Once, when the insect reared up, I banged my head into the ceiling, and I saw stars. But I held on.

And through all of the crashing and banging, through all of the smashing and breaking, through the barking and snarling of Bo, came a new sound:

Sirens.

First one, then another. And one more. These were followed by another distinct sound, a *chopchopchopchopchop,* a heavy whirring that thumped the air.

A helicopter.

Then, as if something was triggered in the ant itself, it backed up with lightning speed. I had to hang on with everything I had and hope I didn't fall off. Soon, the creature was in the living room, then he was bolting toward the front door with me riding on his back, clinging around his neck, hanging on with everything I had . . . about to go on the wildest rodeo ride of my life.

27

Now, when I say the wildest rodeo ride of my life, I *mean* it. Of course, I'd never been in a rodeo before, and the only horse I'd ever ridden was on a carousel at the county fair when I was little. So, I really didn't have any experience on a bucking bronco, and I had no idea what to do now . . . except hold on.

With me on its back, the ant turned in the living room and charged out the front door. I was vaguely aware of Bo behind us, still all riled up and growling fiercely. He was completely fearless, completely unaware that he was after something that was much bigger, stronger, and more powerful than he was.

Outside in the yard, the sirens and the helicopter sounds became louder, but I couldn't see them yet. My main concern was holding onto the ant, keeping a good grip, making sure I didn't fall off.

In the yard, other ants scrambled about. One had succeeded in overturning Mrs. Simms' car! It was upside down in the driveway like a giant steel turtle.

The sirens grew louder. Above, a helicopter zipped past, its blades chopping the air, its motor droning like an enormous June bug. I knew that the rescue vehicles would be there within moments, that help was almost there. All I had to do was hang on.

With Bo in pursuit, the ant charged to a tree in the yard. I held on around the creature's neck tighter than ever. The robot-insect began climbing, working its way up through the branches. In no time at all, I was twenty feet off the ground. I couldn't help but think back to earlier in the day when I had grabbed a branch high in the tree, and it had snapped off. I had been lucky then, as I'd been able to catch another branch. That had broken my fall, and I hadn't tumbled to my death.

Now it was a different story. The only thing I

had to hang onto was this silly ant, climbing higher and higher into the tree. I tried to remember that I was a good tree climber, that I was confident hanging on the branches, weaving through limbs and swinging around trunks like a monkey.

But I wasn't the one in control at the moment. It was the ant. Sure, he was probably a good climber, but if he fell, I would fall with him. What then? Most likely, he would land on top of me. I would be squished as flat as a pancake. Probably flatter.

And so, I made up my mind. I wasn't going to wait for that to happen. I was going to end this ride, and end it then and there.

Above, I saw a branch that I thought would support my weight. If the ant climbed just a little higher, I'd be able to grab hold of it. From there, I would loop myself over it and grab another branch, making my way to the other side of the tree where I would begin to scurry down. Maybe by then the emergency vehicles would arrive. Maybe by then, there would be people on the scene to help me.

Below me, at the base of the tree, Bo had gone absolutely insane. His bark sounded like a mix of anger, frustration, and worry. He wasn't able to climb the tree, and it probably maddened him that he couldn't follow the ant up into the branches.

Then, to my horror, a large brown ant scurried over to the dog, and Bo had no idea that the thing was there. The huge ant reared back, then lunged forward and seized the dog. Bo yelped and cried out, but could do nothing. The ant, gripping the dog tightly with its front legs, scurried away. For the second time that day, Bo had been snared by an ant, and this time, I had a terrible feeling he wasn't going to be so lucky.

The ant I was clinging to climbed up another few feet and made a swift turn to climb onto a branch. It paused for a moment, and I realized that I had my chance. The limb above my head was in reach, and I reached up with one hand and grasped it. With my grip firm, I released my other hand from the neck of the insect, reached up, and grabbed the limb.

From there, it would've been easy for me to simply pull myself up onto the branch. I could have done it without any problem.

However, now I was mad. I think I was madder than I have ever been in my life. I was mad at the ants, or whatever they were. Particularly, I was mad at the ant that had taken my friend, Bo.

So, instead of pulling myself up on the branch, instead of trying to get myself to safety, I pressed my feet against the back of the ant. Still holding the branch above, I pushed the ant as hard as I could, hoping that maybe, just *maybe,* it might be enough to knock him from the tree.

Have you ever done something and immediately realized that it was a horrible idea?

Well, that happened to me at that very moment. When I pushed the ant with my feet, the creature raised one leg and tried to grab a limb. He failed, but he succeeded in catching my left foot.

Knocked off balance from my push, the ant tumbled from the tree. Unable to pull my foot away, the weight of the ant dragged me down. I couldn't hold onto the branch above. My grip slipped, and the ant and I were suddenly in a free fall, headed to the ground some thirty feet below.

28

Although emergency vehicles had started to arrive, I hadn't noticed them. How could I? I was falling faster and faster toward the ground, where I would most likely crack open my skull when I hit the ground. I realized that police cars had started to arrive when I saw lights flashing and found myself on the ground, looking up.

What had happened? Where was I?

For a moment, I was disoriented and scared. Next to me was some giant ant-creature, and he was smoking and making crackling sounds. Sparks were flying everywhere. One hit my cheek, and it burned.

I rolled to the side, and my shoulder cried out in pain. More lights were flashing, and I heard voices over megaphones, the electrical coughing of radios, men and women yelling.

I sat up and watched the flurry of events taking shape around me. A helicopter hovered overhead, red fire trucks were squealing to hurried stops. Several other vehicles were arriving, and a man started barking orders on a megaphone, and his voice—

—was the voice of my dad!

As I was getting to my feet, I spotted him. He was wearing his work clothes—a dark suit and a tie—and he was holding a cone-shaped megaphone. When he saw me, he froze. Then, he dropped the megaphone to the ground and came rushing toward me.

All over the place, other men and women were getting out of vehicles. Some had uniforms, others didn't. A man and a woman saw me and started hustling toward me with a stretcher.

"Scott!" my dad shouted, and it sounded odd to hear him call me by my given name and not my nickname.

I took a step back from the smoldering insect, away from the sparks and smoke. By now it had caught fire, but a group of men were already approaching with fire extinguishers.

"Are you all right?!?!" Dad asked as he ran up to me. He dropped to one knee and placed both hands on my shoulders.

"Yeah," I said, still a little dazed. "I think so. My shoulder hurts."

I moved my left arm, and Dad gave my shoulder a gentle squeeze.

"I think you just twisted it," he said. "You'll be fine. But you're okay, other than your shoulder?"

I nodded, and I looked around.

None of the ants were moving. All of them had frozen in place, and now they looked like statues, like stone skeletons in a museum.

"What happened?" I asked Dad. "Where did those things come from? Mrs. Simms said that they aren't alive, that they're some sort of mechanical robots."

"I'll explain later," Dad said. "Right now, I've got a lot of things to do. You sure you're okay?" he repeated.

"Yeah," I said.

Dad hustled off just as Connor and Annie ran up to me.

"I can't believe you did that!" Connor exclaimed. "I mean . . . that was amazing! You rode on the back of that ant all the way up to the top of that tree!"

"When you fell, we thought it was going to be the end of you," Annie said. "And yet, you walked away from it!"

Mrs. Simms joined us in her yard.

"That was some fall you took, Scott," she said. "Are you all right?"

"Yeah," I said. "I'm fine. Really, I am."

The four of us stood in silence for a moment while the emergency crews went to work. Dad was busy talking to policemen and a few other official-looking men and women. Some trucks arrived carrying forklifts. Men scrambled into the forklifts, drove them off the backs of trucks, and used them to pick up the ants. The insects were then piled onto still more trucks, and when they were loaded full, they were taken away.

"Did your dad tell you what was going on?"

Annie asked.

I shook my head. "No," I replied. "He said he would tell me later, that he was too busy right now."

Truthfully, I really didn't care what had happened. Oh, I guess I was curious and all that. And yes, I felt very lucky. I was alive, and so were my friends. As far as we knew, no one had been hurt.

Except for my best friend, Bo.

A television news crew showed up, and they interviewed us, asking us tons of questions about what had happened. We answered as best we could, but being that we really didn't know exactly what had gone on, or where the ants had come from, we didn't have too much to say. They seemed amazed that we were still alive, and after they left, Connor and Annie talked about how exciting it was going to be to see themselves on the news later that evening.

But that's not what I thought about. I thought about Bo, how he had been so brave, only to be snared by that ant and taken away. I had no idea what happened to him or the ant, but I was sure that it wasn't good.

Mom came home from her friend's, and she was all freaked out. She calmed down after she found out what had happened and that everyone was okay. My little sister, Elise, held tightly to my mom's hand as Mom talked to Dad. By then, all of the robot-insects had been carried off. Elise was fascinated with the flashing red and blue lights, and she kept pointing at them and giggling.

Some repairmen came and began fixing the damage to our home and Mrs. Simms' home. They didn't do much besides cover the holes with plywood, but they did attach a new front door, and one for Mrs. Simms. They would still have a lot of work to do, but they wanted to get all of the holes covered so no wild animals could get in.

Later that day, after all of the emergency vehicles had left, after everyone had gone, we searched all over for Bo. We hiked through the woods, and we went everywhere that Bo traveled. Even Mom helped in the search, even though I knew she really didn't like the dog.

We didn't find him.

29

I took a shower that evening and tried not to think about Bo. After all: he'd been taking care of himself for a long time, probably his whole life. He really didn't have anywhere to go, and he was used to foraging for his own food. I kept telling myself that he was fine.

Unless that robot-insect did something to him, I thought.

Dad was still at work, and he'd told Mom that he would be late, being that there had been the emergency and everything that happened that day. I asked Mom if she knew what happened, but her answers were clouded, and she didn't say very much. She just told me that Dad would explain everything when he got home. I knew that she knew more than she was telling me.

Annie called, and so did Connor. They both wanted to talk about what had happened earlier in the day, and they both wanted to know if I had seen anything of Bo. I told them that I hadn't, but I was going to look for him the next day. They said they'd help.

Dad didn't make it home until around seven o'clock that evening, and he brought pizza for all of us. By then, I was starving. When his car pulled into the driveway, little Elise raced out to meet him. Dad scooped her up with one arm, gave her a hug and a kiss, and then set her back down. I had been sitting on the porch, waiting and watching, thinking.

Dad pulled a large pizza box from the car, walked up to the porch, and sat next to me. The pizza smelled scrumptious, and I was glad that Dad opened up the box right then and there.

"Want some?" he asked with a smile, knowing full well that I love pizza and that I must have been really hungry.

Without responding, I reached into the box and pulled out a triangular slab. It was hot, but that didn't keep me from biting off a huge, gooey chunk.

"Well," Dad said as he helped himself to a slice of pizza. "I suppose it's time you knew the truth about my job, the truth about where I work and what I do."

Dad explained that yes, he worked for a computer software company, but there was a lot more to it than that. The company was designing special robots to be used for search and rescue missions, robots that could go places no human could go. They were designed to be able to save people's lives without endangering the lives of rescuers.

"In our studies, we realized that the ant has all of the features needed to be a super-rescuer," Dad said. "They're strong, and because of their six legs, they're capable of going places and doing things many insects can't.

"We've had a crew of scientists and designers working on these prototypes for a couple of years," Dad continued. "They're specifically made for rescue operations that would put normal human lives in danger."

"But how could a machine replace a human?" I

asked.

"Well, our creation might not be able to *replace* humans," Dad said, "but they could be invaluable in situations that are extremely dangerous. Think about it: Let's say someone is rock climbing, has an accident, and needs to be rescued. If they're in a dangerous location, say a ledge far up on a mountain, humans would risk their lives trying to save that person."

"But one of these robot-ants could do it?" I asked.

Dad nodded. "Exactly. And if something goes wrong and the robot falls, well, we've lost only a machine and not a human life."

I nodded in understanding and took another bite of my pizza.

"I never told you about this because the project is supposed to be top-secret," Dad said. "We've got to be careful, because there are other software companies that want to replicate our design."

"You mean *steal* it?" I asked.

Dad nodded. "I guess you could say that," he said.

We watched Elise play in the yard for a moment. She'd found a butterfly, and she was running all over trying to catch it.

"We call these robots Armored Nonhuman Tactical Searchers," Dad continued. "The acronym, of course, is ANTS. A well-fitting name for a creature that looks like a giant ant, wouldn't you say?"

"For sure," I said. "But what happened? Why did they go crazy and come after us?"

"We've built hundreds of models," Dad continued. "They all run from a software program I've been developing. However, the program is far from perfect. For whatever reason, a glitch in the programming allowed each computer in each individual unit to operate on its own. The ANTS did exactly what they were supposed to do . . . it's just that there was no one giving them direction. That's one of the problems these days. All this new technology is really great, but sometimes, the experiments get out of hand. Sometimes, computer glitches can cause enormous problems."

I knew what he meant. Not long ago, I'd heard about a dinosaur park in South Dakota where some problems with the computers caused a disaster in Rapid City. But I never thought anything like that could happen here, so close to our home.

"We found a room underneath the ground that had a bunch of those things in it," I said. "We thought it was their nest. We thought they were sleeping."

Dad nodded and took another bite of his pizza. "That's our underground storage unit," he explained. "A large utility elevator connects it to our software laboratories. When the ANTS began the malfunction, one of them chewed through the cement wall and burrowed into the earth. That's how they got out. That's what started this whole mess."

I told Dad that Connor and I had fled to the swamp, thinking that the creatures were real, and hoped they wouldn't follow us into the water.

"That was a great idea," Dad said. "Although you couldn't have known it, none of our units are designed to go into water. Not yet, anyway. We're working on several units that will be completely submersible. They'll be able to go into the water, if necessary."

"But why would robots carry a radio?" I asked, and I explained to Dad that one of the ANTS had been carrying what looked like a handheld communication device.

"That's not for the ANTS to communicate," Dad

explained. "That's for the victim. If the person being rescued is conscious, the ANTS can provide them with a radio to put them in contact with emergency medical technicians."

"Oh," I said. "I guess that makes sense."

I helped myself to another piece of pizza.

"We have to make sure we save some of this for your mother and sister," Dad said as he helped himself to another piece.

"I shot one of the things with some arrows," I told Dad. "It stopped him for a minute, but he kept coming after us."

"It's possible that you may have short-circuited a few wires with the arrows," Dad replied. "Still, even if you shot him a dozen times, it probably wouldn't have stopped him."

"This all sounds like one of my science fiction books," I said.

Dad laughed. "When I was your age, I loved reading science fiction. But what was once science fiction is quickly becoming science fact."

He looked around at our house, at the holes in the walls that would have to be fixed, at the debris scattered all over the yard.

All caused by robotic insects, I thought.

"Did they find all of them?" I asked.

"All of the ANTS?" Dad asked.

"Yeah."

"No, not yet," Dad replied. "Once we found out what was going on, we were able to use a special radio frequency to override the computer system inside of each of the ANTS. It automatically shut down each unit, wherever it was, whatever it was doing. We have crews right now going through the woods searching for the few that haven't been accounted for."

I didn't ask Dad if anyone had seen any sign of Bo. It was pointless to ask him about the dog, as he had other things to worry about. Besides: I'd already asked him countless times if I could keep Bo, and he always said the same thing.

No way.

When I crawled into bed that night, I was exhausted, but my mind was still spinning. So much had happened during the day, so many different twists and turns and scary things. I knew if I didn't write it all down, I'd forget everything. I decided that, first thing in the morning, I would grab a pen and a piece of paper and jot down everything I could remember. Like

Annie had said: if my teacher at school asked us to write a story about what happened over the summer, I would have a head start.

And as I closed my eyes, I thought about giant ANTS. I thought about falling out of a tree and Annie being kidnapped. I thought about going down into the tunnel and about the water moccasin that threatened us in the swamp. I thought about the ANTS crawling on our house, chewing through the wall.

But I fell asleep thinking about the ANTS that were still in the forest and around the swamps, the ones that had yet to be found. Even though Dad said they were now no longer active, I dreamed that they really *were* alive, that they were stalking the forest at night, waiting for all of us humans to go to bed.

And at three in the morning, when there was a loud scratching sound beneath my window, I knew that I wasn't dreaming. I knew that, somehow, one of those ANTS had come alive . . . and he was coming for me.

30

When I first heard the scratching, I sat upright in bed. I nearly screamed, but I think I was too frightened, too frozen in terror.

Scratch.

Scrit-Scratch.

The thing was right outside my bedroom window, scratching on the wood panel that had been hastily nailed to the wall to repair the damage caused by the ANTS.

Scratch. Scratch.

I opened my mouth and was about to yell for Mom and Dad when I heard another sound.

A whimper.

Could it be? I wondered excitedly as I threw back the covers and leapt from my bed. *Could it be true?*

As quietly as I could, I hurried out of my bedroom, down the hallway, and through the living room. I opened the front door. Warm air washed over my face, and a zillion crickets and bugs sang a chorus of chiming static.

"Bo?" I quietly called out. "Is that you?"

I heard movement and panting, and my hopeful heart soared. In the darkness, I could make out Bo's dark form bounding toward me. I knelt down and scooped him into my arms. He didn't smell the best, but I didn't care. I was just glad that he was alive.

Without even thinking about what Mom and Dad would say about it, I let Bo inside. I snuck him into my bedroom, and he laid on a rug at the foot of my bed, as if it had always been his very own sleeping spot.

"You sure are a brave dog," I whispered, and I hugged him again before climbing into bed. I fell asleep, and so did Bo.

I had no more nightmares.

ooo

As you probably suspected, Mom and Dad let me keep Bo. I gave him a bath the very first day, and I used some money I'd saved to get him a new blue collar. He follows me everywhere, except, of course, to school. When school started again in the fall, I had to leave him at home. But every day, he waits for me on the porch. When he sees me walking up the road after school, he races to greet me. He really is one of my very best friends, and I'll never forget how brave he was on that very terrifying day when we were attacked by giant insects . . . creatures that weren't really alive at all, but robots called ANTS. Mechanical machines that had gone haywire.

In the spring, Dad got transferred. He was still going to work for the same company, but they were moving him to Iowa, a state far from Alabama.

Which meant, of course, that we *all* moved . . . including Bo.

At first, I didn't like Iowa. I missed my friends,

and I missed the woods and swamps. We moved to the city of Altoona, which is northeast of Des Moines, where Dad's new office was located. We were surrounded by houses, fields, and farmland. It was a lot different from where we'd been living in Alabama.

But I made new friends pretty fast. One of them was a girl in my class named Kayla Blaisdale. When I told her I was from Alabama, she was fascinated.

One day when we were sitting on the swings during our lunch hour, she was asking me about what it was like in Alabama.

"Did you ever get attacked by an alligator?" she asked. "My cousin told me there are lots of alligators in Alabama."

I shook my head. "No," I replied. "Where I lived, there aren't very many alligators. They're usually farther south."

Kayla seemed really interested to hear about what it was like in Alabama, and when I told her what had happened to me, about the ANTS and the panic they'd caused, her jaw dropped.

"I saw that on the news!" she said. "That happened to *you?*"

I nodded. "Yeah," I replied. "Well, me and my

friends. And Bo, my dog."

Kayla asked me a ton of questions about that horrifying day, and I answered them as best I could.

"Wow," she said. "Nothing like that ever happens around here," she said. "Except, of course, last July. But it had nothing to do with robots or anything like that."

"What do you mean?" I asked.

"Have you ever heard of a company called *Incredible Ivy?"* Kayla asked.

I thought about it. "No," I said, shaking my head. "I don't think so."

"That doesn't matter," Kayla replied. "What matters is that it was an experiment that went horribly wrong, and the ivy came to life. Like, the plants had minds of their own."

"You've got to be kidding!" I said. "That had to be *really* scary!"

Kayla nodded. "It was," she said. "But it was even scarier because it happened to me and my friend, Jarvis DeMotte."

"You mean this ivy actually came to *life?"* I asked. "You *saw* this?"

Again, Kayla nodded. "Not only did I see it, but

the plants attacked me and Jarvis. We were lucky we weren't killed."

The lunch bell rang, and it was time to go back to class.

"Tell you what," Kayla said as she got up from the swing. "Meet me back here after school, and I'll tell you all about it. I'll tell you everything that happened."

For the rest of the day, I couldn't concentrate on my schoolwork. I barely heard the teacher talking. All I could think about was what had happened to Kayla. I couldn't wait to hear her story.

Later, after school, I met Kayla on the playground, and she shared what had happened to her and Jarvis in July of last year. Kayla told me all about her experience with the nightmarish ivy that came alive, slithering through the field like bloodthirsty, green snakes, looking for their next victim . . . .

Next:

AMERICAN
CHILLERS
AMERICA'S #1 SERIES FOR MAXIMUM CHILLS!

#40: Incredible Ivy of Iowa

Continue on for a FREE preview!

1

"There it is," I said to Jarvis, with my finger against the glass of the store window. "That's the bike I'm going to get."

Jarvis took one look at the bike and turned to face me. He was frowning, his eyes were wide, and his playful grin said it all: he didn't believe me. He didn't think there was any way I would be able to afford the bike.

"It's a cool-looking bike, Kayla," he said, nodding toward the window. "But you told me that your parents aren't going to buy it for you. Where are *you* going to get the money?"

"I'll get a job, and I'll earn it," I replied confidently.

"Kayla," Jarvis said, again nodding toward the bicycle on the other side of the glass. "That bicycle is almost three hundred dollars. Where are you going to get a job that earns that kind of money? You're 11 years old."

"You wait and see," I said, putting my hands on my hips. "I'll get it."

"You'd be a lot better off saving your money for something like this," Jarvis said, and he pulled out his new pocket knife to show me. I knew that he'd wanted it, and he's been saving his money since earlier in the year. It was a Swiss Army knife, and it had not only a blade, but nearly a dozen other useful tools that folded neatly within the handle.

"That's a nice pocket knife," I said, "but it

only cost thirty dollars. My bike costs a lot more."

Jarvis returned the knife to his pocket, and I took another long look at the bicycle. It was candy apple red with big, knobby tires for tearing through trails. The seat and handlebars were black, and it was the coolest looking bicycle I'd ever seen. It certainly was a lot better than the old bike that I was still riding around, the bike that had been my brother's before he outgrew it.

"Well," Jarvis said. "Good luck. I mean, it's a very cool bicycle and all, but that's a lot of money to earn in only one summer."

And it was. The exact price of the bike was two hundred ninety-nine dollars, and I still hadn't figured out how to get all that money. I thought about babysitting, I thought about lemonade stands and bake sales. I thought about mowing lawns, I thought about anything to earn enough money to buy the bicycle. And although I couldn't really come up with anything right away, I refused to give up. I refused to give up dreaming. I refused to think that I wouldn't be able to earn the money.

I knew I could.

I knew I *would*.

And I was certain, beyond any shadow of a doubt, that I would have enough money to buy the bicycle before the end of the summer.

I just didn't know that it might cost me my life—and Jarvis' life—to get it.

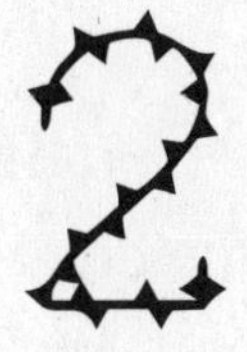

When I got home that afternoon, there was a strange vehicle in the driveway. It was a green pickup truck. On the driver's side door were the words *Incredible Ivy* printed in white letters. There was a phone number beneath it, and the words and telephone number were circled with what appeared to be vines of some sort, colored red and yellow. I hadn't seen the truck before, and I wondered if it belonged to a friend of one of my parents.

I parked my old bicycle in the garage and went into the house. My dad was standing in the living room talking to a man I hadn't seen before. He was tall and thin with short black hair peppered with gray. Dad and the man looked at me when I came in.

"And here she is, right now," my dad said. "Mr. Nelson, this is my daughter, Kayla."

The man named Mr. Nelson extended his hand, and I extended mine. We shook.

"Hi," I said.

Mr. Nelson eyes sparkled. "It's very nice to meet you, Miss Blaisdale," he said.

I was a little surprised, a little embarrassed. No one had ever called me Miss Blaisdale. Everyone calls me by my first name, Kayla.

"Mr. Nelson is a friend of mine from a long time ago," my dad explained. "He's opening a business not far away, and he's looking for people who are interested in a little part-time work."

"That's right," Mr. Nelson said with a nod. "Your father tells me you've been looking to earn some money."

"Um, yeah," I said. "I've been trying to think of ways, but nothing is really coming to mind. And I'm too young to have an official part-time job."

"Well," Mr. Nelson continued, "you're certainly not too young to help me out around my farm. That is, of course, if you're interested."

"Yeah, sure," I said, not bothering to even ask what kind of work he wanted me to do. I was just so excited at the chance to earn some money that it didn't matter. At that point, I would've done anything.

"There's a lot of work that needs to be done," Mr. Nelson said, "and I might be looking for someone else. Do you have a friend who would also like to earn a little extra money?"

Without even thinking, I nodded my head and spoke.

"I'll bet my friend, Jarvis DeMotte, would love to earn some money."

Mr. Nelson frowned, and his look became serious. "Is he a good worker? Your father tells me that you work very hard, and that's good. But how about your friend? Does he work as hard as you?"

Again, I nodded. "Jarvis would be a great worker," I said. "And I know that he would love to earn some extra money."

"Perfect!" Mr. Nelson said, clasping his hands together and rubbing his palms. "Do you think you and Jarvis could come to my farm tomorrow? I can show you around, and you can even start working in the afternoon."

I thought about this for a moment. The next day was Friday, and I didn't have anything going on. It was June, and school had just got out for the summer, so I didn't have that to worry about. And even if I did have something going on, I would change it, especially now that I had a real paying job!

"That would be great!" I said excitedly. "I'll call Jarvis right now and let him know."

"My farm is only a couple of miles away,"

Mr. Nelson said. "You and your friend can probably ride your bicycles there. I'll draw you a map, but it's very easy to find. And be sure to wear old clothing, because you're going to get dirty.""

Mr. Nelson and my dad continued talking, and I excused myself to my bedroom. I grab my phone and immediately call Jarvis.

"Guess what?" I asked.

"What?" Jarvis replied.

"We have jobs!" I said.

"What do you mean?" Jarvis asked.

"Just that!" I said. "There's a guy here, he's a friend of my dad's, and he wants us to work at his farm. We need to be there tomorrow at noon."

Jarvis paused. "You mean like a job that pays *money?*"

"Yes!" I answered.

Again, Jarvis paused. "What do we have to do?"

"Who cares?" I said. "It's a job. We're going to earn money."

"How much?" Jarvis asked.

"I don't know that, either," I said. "But it's a job, Jarvis! We're going to earn money. I'm going to earn enough for my bicycle, just like I said!"

Jarvis agreed to meet me at my house at 11:30 the next day. From there, we'd ride our bikes to Mr. Nelson's farm. And while I had no idea what duties the job required, I didn't care. I would do anything. Mr. Nelson had told me to wear old clothes, so I figured most of the work would be outside.

I was so excited that night that I had a hard time falling asleep. I read for a long time, and then I put my book down and turned off the light. I closed my eyes, but it seemed like they kept opening on their own. I turned the light on again and read some more, then turned off the light again and put my book on the stand beside my bed.

A job, I thought, as I lay awake in bed, my head resting on the pillow. My bedroom window was open, and the soothing sound of crickets drifted through the screen.

A real, honest to goodness, paying job. I'm going to get that bicycle, for sure.

I finally fell asleep, dreaming about my new bicycle, dreaming about speeding over trails, through puddles, and through the woods. All of this I imagined in my mind . . . But I never imagined the terrible things that were about to happen Jarvis and me at a small farm called *Incredible Ivy*.

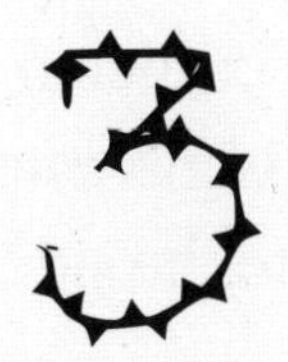

"I never knew this place was here," Jarvis said, turning his head from left to right.

We were on our bikes, stopped at a big, green gate. A sign on it read:

STOP! PROPERTY OF INCREDIBLE IVY. NO TRESPASSING.

The gate was locked.

"My dad said that the place is pretty new,"

I said. "I guess some of the buildings have been here for a while, and some others are new. But as far as the farm goes, it was built by Mr. Nelson."

I had my phone in my back pocket, and I pulled it out to check the time. It was 11:55 AM. We were five minutes early.

However, as I returned the phone to my pocket, I heard tires crunching gravel. Jarvis and I turned to see Mr. Nelson's truck coming toward us. We rolled our bikes to the side of the driveway and waited.

We spent the next hour following Mr. Nelson as he gave us a tour of the farm. First of all, he showed us the ivy. Some of the vines were green, some were red. He explained that the green plants were males, and the red plants were females.

"I didn't even know there was such a thing as male and female plants," I said.

"It's not uncommon at all," said Mr. Nelson.

Then, he showed us the warehouse that was used for storing equipment and farming machinery. Inside was a large tractor that was identical to the kind my dad has. It was green and yellow, and taller than me. When I was little, Dad used to give me rides around our yard and in the field in the back. When I got bigger he showed me how to drive it, and once in a while, he lets me take it out by myself.

Mr. Nelson then took us to see the irrigation building, which was basically an old, red barn. Inside was an ancient, blue pickup truck covered with a film of chalky, gray dust. The truck looked like it hadn't been driven in years.

There was also a very large, fifty-gallon drum labeled *WEED KILLER* behind the truck. It, too, was covered with dust.

On the wall on the other side of the truck was a sickle with a rusty blade. A sickle is a long tool, the size of a garden shovel. But instead of having a blade to dig a hole, it has a long, curved sword for cutting down tall grass and brush.

But the most impressive thing about the irrigation building? An enormous silver tank, three times the size of the truck. It sat right outside of the red barn like a giant, steel aquarium.

"This is a 5,000 gallon irrigation tank," Mr. Nelson explained, rapping on the metal with a bare knuckle. "This is where all of the water is pumped from the ground and is stored before it goes into the field. It's where we mix my special fertilizer with water. Each day, I add five gallons of liquid fertilizer to this tank, and only five gallons."

The fertilizer was stored in five gallon containers next to the barn. They were made of yellow plastic, and labeled *Warning! Incredible Ivy fertilizer. Handle with care!*

While we watched, Mr. Nelson poured one of the five gallon containers of fertilizer into the giant tank, which was exactly like pouring gasoline into any engine.

"But what's so special about the ivy?" I asked. It was a question that I had been burning to ask Mr. Nelson since the day before.

"Ah, yes," Mr. Nelson replied. "I've been working on this for several years. I've been able to successfully graft several plants together, including ivy, broccoli, asparagus, and spinach. What I've created is a hybrid plant that grows very fast. But best of all, it's nearly 100% nutritionally complete. My Incredible Ivy contains all essential vitamins and minerals, and it's loaded with protein, carbohydrates, and fats that can sustain human life for months and months."

"You mean," Jarvis said, his eyes widening, "you can *live* on this stuff?" he asked, and he made a sweeping gesture with his arm that encompassed the field of red and green ivy. "I mean, if that's all I ate, I wouldn't have to eat anything else?"

Mr. Nelson nodded. "For a good long time, yes," he replied. "Of course, you'd still have to drink water, as no human being can go for more than a few days without water. But think of the possibilities! If my ivy farm is successful, we can duplicate plantations in other countries where food is badly needed. No one will ever have to starve again! My Incredible Ivy will go a long way toward eliminating world hunger."

Wow! I thought. *How exciting! Jarvis and I*

are part of a project that's going to make a huge difference in the world!

"I've been working on this project—"

Mr. Nelson suddenly stopped speaking. His jaw fell. His eyes bulged, and he looked over my shoulder.

"Look out!" he screamed. *"Get down!"*

Mr. Nelson fell to his knees and covered his head with his hands. Not knowing what to expect, the only thing Jarvis and I could do was get down and prepare for the worst . . . whatever that would be.

ABOUT THE AUTHOR

Johnathan Rand has been called 'one of the most prolific authors of the century.' He has authored more than 75 books since the year 2000, with well over 4 million copies in print. His series include the incredibly popular **AMERICAN CHILLERS, MICHIGAN CHILLERS, FREDDIE FERNORTNER, FEARLESS FIRST GRADER**, and **THE ADVENTURE CLUB.** He's also co-authored a novel for teens (with Christopher Knight) entitled **PANDEMIA**. When not traveling, Rand lives in northern Michigan with his wife and three dogs. He is also the only author in the world to have a store that sells only his works: **CHILLERMANIA!** is located in Indian River, Michigan and is open year round. Johnathan Rand is not always at the store, but he has been known to drop by frequently. Find out more at:

www.americanchillers.com

All AudioCraft books are proudly printed, bound, and manufactured in the United States of America, utilizing American resources, labor, and materials.

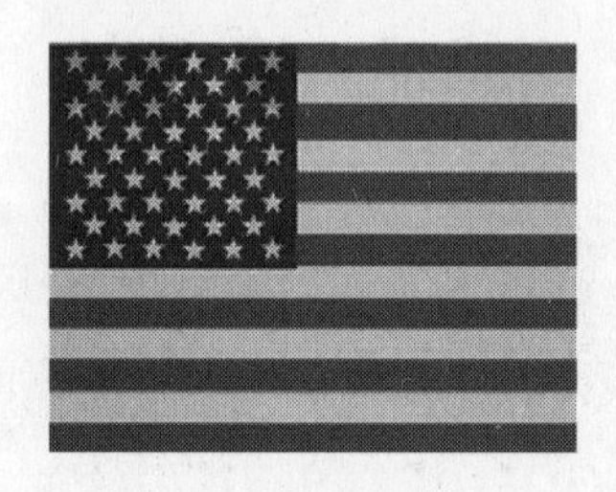

USA